Tropical Swap

Laurence Shames

ISBN: 1507815409
ISBN-13: 978-1507815403

DEDICATION

To Marilyn,
The mate that fate had me created for

Works by Laurence Shames

Key West Novels—

Tropical Swap

Shot on Location

The Naked Detective

Welcome to Paradise

Mangrove Squeeze

Virgin Heat

Tropical Depression

Sunburn

Scavenger Reef

Florida Straits

Key West Short Fiction—

Chickens

New York and California Novels—

Money Talks

The Angels' Share

Nonfiction—

The Hunger for More

The Big Time

Part 1

1.

For Meg and Peter Kaplan, the home exchange was going perfectly well, wonderfully really, until the coconut crashed through the window at three a.m.

They were sleeping upstairs when it happened. The window shattered by the coconut was downstairs. Muffled by distance and humidity, by tasteful rugs and fluffy pillows, the sounds of the splintering and the thud were abrupt and sharp but not terribly loud. Meg and Peter only half woke up and only for a groggy moment.

They'd gone to bed extremely tired, worn out from dragging luggage through airport security lines and from the shock of sudden searing sunshine in February. It had been seventeen degrees under a vacant sky when they left their Manhattan apartment that morning; by the time they'd landed in Key West, the thermometer stood at eighty-two and the yellow sun seemed so close and unshielded that they imagined they could see it spinning. The winter heat was thrilling but confusing to their bodies, which had opened toward the light like hungry plants but then had quickly wilted.

By next morning they barely remembered that anything untoward had happened in the night.

Warm as biscuits, they woke up in an unaccustomed bed to the lush and slightly raunchy smells of the near-tropics—the funk of wet fallen foliage, the narcotic fog of flowers just being born, the jungle tang of spray from the neighborhood cats—and moment by moment they recalled where they were: In yet another stranger's house on yet another home swap.

Experienced exchangers, they had never yet grown numb to the fundamental oddness of the process, nor to the remarkable optimism on which it needed to be based. Home exchanging was all about trust—trust that one's swap partner was not a total slob, scam artist, lunatic, or violent criminal. But how could people like the Kaplans know if they'd placed their trust wisely? They looked at some photos on a website and then there they were, not just in someone else's house, but smack dab in the middle of a life that other people had made; surrounded not just by other people's stuff, but by their choices, passions, personality. What did these or those people choose to display, to highlight? Family photos, gewgaws, bowling trophies? Were there books? Was there art? Deer heads on the walls? Were there ships in bottles or needlepoint pillows with homey sayings? Everything, even the refrigerator magnets, seemed to be a fragment of an entirely present though still elusive story.

Then there was the inevitable locked closet, which, in this case, seemed to be the husband's half of a his-and-hers pair in the master bedroom, the wife's half having been left open, with a good amount of space considerately cleared. In any case, every home they'd ever exchanged for had had a locked closet somewhere, and it invariably became a subject of mystery. The locked closet was like some repressed subconscious with hangers and drawers. What were people hiding in those musty and perhaps guilty chambers? Chances are, their contents were generally quite mundane: the better china, the aging Burgundies, the heirloom pony glasses from Alsace. No doubt the locked rooms also sometimes hid the sex toys, the stash of naughty videos, the home bondage starter kit in its cheesy vinyl case. Harmless though somewhat embarrassing stuff. But who could say with certainty that there might not on occasion be some truly insidious things shut away behind those closet doors? Firearms, explosives, blackmail-worthy photographs, records of embezzlements or frauds or even murder—who knew?

Short of breaking in to those locked closets, which of course was something that people like the Kaplans would never, ever do, they couldn't fully know the sudden friends whose beds they were sleeping in, whose sinks and towels they were using, whose toothbrush holders were now cradling their own toothbrushes.

And who, in turn, were resident in *their* home, sizing them up by their possessions and their style, and wondering about them as well.

But about the coconut...

It wasn't until after Meg and Peter had showered and dressed that they came downstairs and saw it. Still shrouded in its fibrous pale green husk, it looked enormous, bigger than any coconut they had ever seen. It was lying in the middle of the living room, the centerpiece in a bizarre mosaic of shattered glass. The glass had fractured mostly into narrow triangles, some of which glinted and some of which didn't. Seeing the mess, the visitors finally remembered hearing the vague and dreamy crash. Meg said, "Was it really so windy last night?"

Peter said, "I didn't think so." He looked at what was left of the window. It was an ordinary window, which is to say, it was oriented vertically. Then he looked at the coconut, which appeared to be quite heavy, five pounds or so, he guessed, and he started to get worried. To worriers all things are worrying, and Peter was a first-class worrier. In airplanes he worried about the slightest change in the sound of the engines. In a car he worried about his tire pressure and whether the gas gauge was telling him the truth. On a bicycle he fretted about chain noise or pinging spokes that might fail and leave him stranded far from home. He worried about floods and droughts, recession and inflation, gaining weight and losing weight. Now he was worried about the trajectory of the coconut. He said, "I don't think there's any way that thing just blew through the window."

His wife pursed her lips, glanced this way and that, and had to agree. "Maybe it fell and bounced off a frond. You know, a slingshot kind of thing. Or trampoline."

She did not sound worried, and she wasn't. She was blithe, she was cheery, she didn't worry about anything. In this and in other things as well, she counterbalanced and completed her husband. Their marriage, a steady and generally happy one, was held together like, say, a loaf of bread, by their quite different personalities. Peter was like the flour and the water; without Meg he would have sat there in a passive, gooey lump. Meg was like the yeast and the salt; without Peter she would have gaily fizzed and frothed until she'd wafted away into her own carefree but somewhat unmoored reality.

She now bent down and started picking up the shards of glass. Worried that she would cut herself, Peter went off in search of a dustpan and a broom.

When a path through the wreckage had been cleared, Peter gingerly stepped forward and picked up the coconut. He weighed it with his hands, then turned it over and blanched. "Oh my God," he said.

"What?"

"There's writing on it."

He carried the coconut over to his wife. She looked at it quickly and saw some vague markings scrawled in waxy red. "They're just squiggles," she said.

"No, here," he insisted, and slowly twirled the coconut to reveal a different facet of its husk. There did in fact seem to be some words there, though the letters were crudely rendered and seemed to have been partly smeared or scraped away when the projectile had crashed through the window. Still, among the crosshatched lines and drips, a short and discomfiting message could be made out: *She dies.* Then, after a space with some other illegible markings, two more words: *You die.*

Meg, unworried, said, "We die, you die, they die. Sounds like someone conjugating verbs."

Peter's throat had tightened down and he now held the coconut very carefully, far away from his body, as though it might explode. His voice pinched and rasping, he managed to say, "No one's conjugating. It's a death threat. Can't you see that? It's a death threat."

"Death threat against who? We just got here. We don't even know anyone."

"Must be against the people whose house it is," reasoned Peter.

"They aren't here," Meg pointed out.

"Probably no one knows they're gone," her husband said. "Probably they'd just left when we walked in. I thought I could still smell after-shave. I don't like this whole business, Meg."

"Come on, it's just a coconut. A prank. A joke."

"Right. A joke. Someone breaks your window and wants to kill you. Ha, ha, ha."

"Honey, no one's killing anyone. It's all fine. We're in Key West. Let's have fun. Let's relax."

Peter did not relax. He gingerly placed the coconut on the kitchen counter and could not stifle a shudder as he let go of it. "These people we're exchanging with," he said. "What do we really know about them?"

2.

The house that Meg and Peter were borrowing was on Poorhouse Lane, a short and very narrow street near the west end of the cemetery. Back in the 1800s there had actually been a poorhouse there, a place where paupers were given soup and sermons and lectures about the presumptive virtues of hard work. Now the lane was one of those patchwork precincts so typical of Key West, with a sprinkling of million-dollar second homes among the peeling and off-plumb cottages occupied by deep locals who would never move or transients camped out in rental units whose landlords had long since ceased to give a damn about the properties. These funkier dwellings were ringed by wobbly chain-link fences enclosing yards where anarchic shrubbery grew in choking tangles. Here and there a clunky old air-conditioner bulged from a sagging window, dripping rusty water and looking like it might pull the whole building down.

By contrast, the home where Meg and Peter found themselves was one of the nicest on the block. It rose two stories tall, straight and proud behind a tidy, freshly-painted picket fence. Its ageless Dade County pine siding gleamed a faultless white that was tastefully set off by shutters of celadon green. The front of the house faced north and featured a deep and shady porch complete with a rocking chair and rope swing. The backyard had a swimming pool that was not quite big enough for actual swimming but was very beckoning nonetheless. In all it was a serene and luxurious accommodation, but Peter Kaplan, even at poolside, was not serene.

"Okay," he said to his wife. "Let's start at the beginning and try to figure out who we're dealing with here. Take it step by step. You contacted these people—"

"No I didn't," Meg corrected. As usual, she had been the one who handled the arrangements, her husband being somewhat overwhelmed in wrapping up a trimester at the not very good New Jersey college where he taught literature. Meg, having neither craved nor stumbled into a conventional career, worked sometimes as a yoga teacher and occasionally in a health food store and now and then in a used book shop. Her schedule was flexible, and besides, it was she who had the travel bug, who was always lobbying to go somewhere while her husband would have just as soon stayed where he was. So it fell to her to put in the time at the computer, to browse the listings, filter the emails. "They contacted us," she said.

"They contacted *us?*" said Peter. They were sitting at a glass-topped wicker table in the dappled shade of a fishtail palm. Meg was drinking coffee from a giant mug. Peter was sipping tea. He'd given up coffee some years before because it made him nervous. Now he drank tea in small doses but was nervous anyway. "Doesn't that strike you as strange?"

"What?"

"That people with a great house in Key West would want to swap for a so-so apartment on West End Avenue."

"It's a nice apartment," Meg protested. "And people love New York. Everybody wants to go there."

"In February?"

"There's so much to do. Theatre, opera, the symphony."

"Old ladies disappearing into slush puddles," said Peter. "Taxis slamming sideways into snowbanks. It's a terrible time to be in New York."

"To each his own," Meg said mildly. "Maybe they had some event to go to. Some special reason to be there."

"Like what?"

"How should I know? All he said in his email—"

"He?"

"Yeah, it was the husband I guess, this guy Benny. All he said was that it was a last minute kind of thing."

"Aha!" said Peter, as though some major point had just been proven.

"Aha what?"

"Last minute kind of thing. Like maybe it wasn't so much about going to New York at all. Maybe it was more about needing to get out of here."

"Peter, please, slow down. The coconut, the broken window, okay, that's a little weird, I admit it. But--"

"And what about the death threat?"

"Stop already with the death threat. You're reading way too much into it."

"Am I? I'm just reading what's on the coconut. *She dies you die.* I don't think it's a big stretch to call that a death threat."

"I still say it's a prank. A random event. At worst maybe some petty vandalism. And have I pointed out that the only people it could possibly have been aimed at aren't even here?"

"Exactly. And you know why they aren't? Because we are. Unsuspecting suckers. Sitting ducks."

Meg placidly sipped her coffee and dropped her voice to the lulling murmur she favored at the end of a yoga class. "Ducks," she said. "Ducks sitting on a pond in sunshine. Isn't that a peaceful image? Or look at the pool, the way the water looks so blue and still. Isn't that beautiful?"

Her husband threw a quick look at the swimming pool, blinked once, and pulled his eyes away. "Or think about it this way. Say you were in trouble. Say someone was after you, you needed to get out of town. How would you do it? Go to a hotel? You go to a hotel, you need a reservation, you need to check in with a credit card. There's a paper trail, people know you're there. But with a home exchange—"

"Now you're getting completely carried away."

"With a home exchange nobody can find you. Perfect way to take it on the lam. Who else knows these people are hiding out on West End Avenue and 93rd Street?"

"Who says they're hiding out?"

"No one knows but us, and I don't like being the only ones who know."

"Peter, breathe. Bring your attention to the center and breathe deeply into it."

"What if somebody comes looking for them and ties us up with duct tape and won't let us go until we tell him where they are? I'd tell him in a minute, don't get me wrong. The idea of being tied up in a chair makes me claustrophobic. But do I want that on my conscience?"

"Look, honey, slow down. It's just a broken window. Happens every day. These are just normal people. Trusting, easygoing home exchangers, our kind of folks. I've spoken on the phone with the guy. He sounded just like a regular person."

"Have you ever spoken on the phone with Charles Manson? Maybe he sounds like a regular person too. How long was the conversation?"

"Not long. Short. A minute. He said he had to go."

"Had to go. See? Sounded jumpy?"

"He didn't sound jumpy. He had another call."

"I'm really not sure we should stay here, Meg."

Meg ran her fingertips along the lip of her coffee mug and looked around the strangers' property. In the half day they'd been there, she'd already fallen in love with many things about it—the banks of skyflower at the far end of the pool, the barely audible whoosh of breeze through palms, the glass block wall that let fractured light into the master suite shower. It all came pretty close to her fantasy of a perfect Key West house and she didn't want to run away from it just because of a thrown coconut. "Listen," she said, "I have a very simple idea. Let's just call this fellow up, calmly tell him about the window, ask him who he uses for glass repairs. He'll apologize for the inconvenience, he'll be very reassuring and it'll all be fine. How's that sound?"

Peter put his teacup down, drummed fingers on the glass tabletop. Finally, with grudging and not more than tentative resignation, he nodded.

So Meg riffled through her contact list until she came to Benny Bufano. She hit the call button and was forwarded to voicemail but it turned out she couldn't leave a message. The mailbox was full. This made Peter nervous.

"Full mailbox," he said. "That's never good. Guy's not checking messages. Things are spinning out of control for him."

Meg just sighed and sent Benny Bufano a text.

Peter, paranoid but in this instance also correct, guessed that it would go unanswered.

3.

While waiting to hear back from Benny Bufano, Meg unfurled her bright blue mat and did some yoga next to the pool. She'd stripped down to her bra and panties, then, realizing that the yard was quite perfectly private, had casually tossed the bra onto a nearby lounge chair. At 47, she was an extremely handsome woman, confident though not aggressive in her posture, easy in her smooth unfussy skin. Her arms and legs were lean and toned, her tummy was flat from all the planks and boat poses, and her smallish breasts were so far holding their own in the ceaseless fight against gravity. Her face could fairly be described as likeable and pert rather than classically beautiful, with a little nose, a playful mouth, and tiny ears unhidden by her stylishly short but above all practical haircut. Her eyes were hazel flecked with yellow, and at moments they seemed to open improbably wide to allow in more of the endlessly surprising spectacle all around her. At poolside now, she stretched and lunged and folded, and her husband watched her for a while with vague but genuine appreciation.

Mixed in with the appreciation was just a touch of envy. Peter, once a pretty decent athlete--a somewhat geeky high school wrestler who had occasionally shocked opponents with sporadic and seemingly out-of-character bursts of scrappiness and even ferocity—would have liked to rest his mind awhile and exercise his body instead; but as usual his worrying got the better of him and he began to fidget.

After a while he left the pool area and walked around to the side yard—the side of the house where the broken window was. He'd decided he needed to inspect the place more closely, though he had no idea what he hoped to learn by doing so. Had there been clues on the ground or in the shrubbery as to who or what had launched the coconut he would have had no idea how to read them. What should he be looking for? Footprints? Strands of hair or garment fibers caught on twigs? He stood there for some moments, chin in hand, trying to appear sagacious, knowing all the while that he was wasting his time.

Then he heard a voice call out from the house next door. "Whatcha looking for?"

He wheeled in the direction of the sound but at first saw no one. The house itself was an appalling shack whose wooden boards had originally overlapped but which had by now been warped and stretched so that there were dim and undulating gaps between them. The house had once been painted blue but all that remained of the paint were some random flecks of color that tenuously clung to the façade like exhausted butterflies. At the front of the shack, propped on cinder blocks, was a sagging porch whose splintery floorboards seemed to tilt in several planes at once. Peering through the gauzy foliage that sprouted between the two wildly unequal houses, Peter finally saw a very old man sitting in a rocker on the porch.

Their eyes met, and the old man called out, "'Lo there, can I help you?"

As a New Yorker, Peter was not accustomed to being so casually and heartily hailed by neighbors, but he tried to find the right tone to respond in kind. "Got a broken window last night," he said.

"Along about three a.m.," the old man said.

"Coconut came crashing through. You heard it?"

"Heard something. I don't sleep that good."

"Trying to figure out how it happened."

The old man said nothing.

Peter said, "See anything?"

"Nope. I don't see that good. You a friend of the Bufanos?"

"Actually, no, not really. We're just here on a home exchange."

"A what?" the old man said. "I don't hear that good. Whyn't ya come over and say hello."

So Peter threaded his way through the plantings between the two yards and climbed a couple of weatherbeaten and untrustworthy stairs to the old man's porch. The old man introduced himself as Mel and motioned his visitor into a creaky wooden chair whose back spindles yielded like loose teeth when he leaned even lightly against them. As he sat he studied his host, who had a face like one of those kitsch sculptures that people used to whittle out of drying apple cores. His bony chin jutted forward in front of a collapsed and lean-lipped mouth. His watery blue eyes were overshadowed by an angular brow that hung down like an awning. He said to Peter, "So you were saying something about a home on the range?"

"No. I said it was a home exchange."

"Ah, home exchange. What's that?"

Peter told him.

"So, like, you mean, you swap houses with somebody and you get to stay someplace for free? I should check into that sometime."

Peter said nothing, just discreetly glanced around him. On defeated hinges hung a screen door that featured an aluminum silhouette of a flamingo. The screen had holes in it. Some of them were patched with cotton balls and some with what appeared to be little wads of toilet paper.

"So anyway," Peter said, "I really don't know the people we're swapping with at all. I'm curious about them. You a friend of theirs?"

"Friend?" said Mel, with a small shrug of his shrunken shoulders. "Just more like neighbors. The woman, Glenda her name is, her I've hardly seen. The guy, Benny, him I know a little bit. Seems like a nice fella. He comes by now and then to chat. Coupla times he brought beers. We drank beer and talked about pussy."

Peter wasn't sure he'd heard correctly and so said nothing.

"Pussy," the old man said again, a little louder, attempting a smile that highlighted his lack of teeth. "That's mainly what I like to talk about. You?"

Peter hesitated then said, "Um, I'm married."

"Yeah, what of it?"

"So, well, pussy just isn't something I would tend to talk about."

"Too bad," said Mel. "Me, I was in the Merchant Marine. Got pussy all over the world. Long stretches in between, of course. So when I finally caught some I had to make it count. Lemme tell ya about this incredible piece of ass I had in Manila in, oh, I guess we're talking 1958."

"No," said Peter. "That's really okay."

The old man went on anyway. "Had the most amazing red-brown skin, like polished wood, like a fancy piece of furniture. Took her panties down and I couldn't believe there wasn't a pale place anywhere."

"Listen, I really don't need to hear this."

"So we're in this tiny room behind the bar, no door, just glass beads, and she starts—"

"Mel, really, I'm happy for you but spare me, okay?"

Peter's tone must have firmed because the old man finally seemed to hear what he was saying. "You really don't like talking pussy?"

Peter said nothing. The old man didn't seem offended, just truly surprised. There was a brief silence save for the creaking of the boards and a soft churring of palm fronds. Then Mel went on, "How 'bout being married. Ya like that?"

Caught a bit off balance by the sudden segue and the directness of the question, Peter stammered slightly before saying, "Well yeah, sure, of course I do."

"Wouldn't'a worked for me," the old man said, shaking his head so that the flaps of loose skin beneath his chin wiggled back and forth. "Too restless. Couldn't sit still... Must be nice, though, having someone there. Someone you can count on."

Peter nodded and suddenly pictured his wife on her blue mat, doing her routine. Having someone there, someone to count on— maybe this lonely old sex fiend had just nailed what marriage was mostly about: Relying on someone, being together in the ordinary, uneventful times, not much being said or needing to be said. Cooking dinner. Reading side by side. Tugging a blanket back and forth in the middle of the night...

"But listen," Peter said, "I'm a little concerned about the broken window. The coconut. I don't think it just fell out of a tree."

"No," said Mel. "They don't usually fall sideways."

"So we agree. You think somebody threw it?"

"Coulda. There's drunks. Kids. People who don't like newcomers or fancy houses in the neighborhood. Stuff happens."

"Serious stuff? Like really serious stuff?"

"This is Key West, my friend. What are we calling serious?"

Peter decided not to offer more detail. He said, "These people, Benny and Brenda—"

"Glenda."

"Benny and Glenda. You think people don't like them? You think they have enemies?"

"You mean besides each other?"

"Excuse me?"

"That's why I asked how you like being married. I was thinking about Benny and Glenda. They didn't seem to like it one damn bit."

"Oh?"

"Used to fight all the time. Constantly. Big arguments. Threats. Yelling. Throwing things. Plates. Toasters. That's why he'd stop by here, to get away from the arguing. You and your wife, you fight much?"

"Hardly ever. And we don't throw things."

"Well, anyway, they split up."

The simple statement puzzled Peter. He'd had a clear if undetailed image of a couple staying in the West End Avenue apartment and now he had to totally revise that image. Off the beat, he said, "So, they're not together?"

"Right. That's what split up means. Don't know if they're divorcing or what, but she finally took off maybe a month ago after one last donnybrook. Screaming, doors slamming, then it got real quiet. Heard she went back to where she used to live. New York."

"New York?" said Peter.

"New York," the old man said again, a little louder. "You got hearing problems too?"

Peter in fact had heard the words perfectly well but they had ramped up his worrying and also slightly shifted its trajectory. He thought again about the cryptic words scrawled on the coconut: *She dies you die.* This was the problem with bad grammar; it left meanings unclear, admitted of alternate readings. Was the intended message she dies *and* you die? Or was it *if* she dies, you die? To Peter this suddenly seemed far more likely. His instantaneous, paranoid but not illogical thought process went something like this: This guy Benny Bufano had a wife with whom he fought like crazy, but they probably would not have bothered fighting unless they really loved each other, and then she left him, which might or might not have been heartbreaking but was a humiliation at the least. She'd bolted to New York. Not long after, Benny, on what he admitted was a last minute impulse, went to New York as well. In February. Leaving his lovely Key West home at the choicest time of year in Florida. Why, except for some desperate purpose, would he do that? Why, unless he'd decided to track down and murder the wife he couldn't live with and couldn't live without? But then there came a complication: In despair and probably drinking heavily, he must have told someone his plan, and that someone, who didn't realize that Benny had just left town, was promising to kill him if he followed through on it? *If* she dies you die. What could be clearer?

Peter, suddenly close to full-blown panic, stood up so abruptly that old Mel flinched in his rocking chair. "You going?"

Already heading down the creaking stairs, Peter said, "Got to think some things through. Got to talk them over with my wife."

"Must be nice," the old man said to his retreating back, "having someone to talk things over with. Well, stop by anytime. We'll talk pussy some more. You'll get to like it, wait and see."

4.

"But that's ridiculous," said Meg.

She'd finished her yoga and was standing in the pool doing some aerobics. Her blue mat had been neatly rolled and put aside and her panties had been tossed onto the lounge chair with her bra. The sun was high by now and sharp yellow sunshine glinted on the water all around her, seeming to raise it into little curls like the tips on icing. The first inklings of a tan were starting to blossom on her neck and shoulders.

Peter was pacing at the edge of the pool. "It's not ridiculous. Tell me why it's ridiculous."

Meg was doing that exercise where you trace out circles with your leg, first one direction then the other, then you switch legs and start the whole thing over. Without interrupting the flow, she said, "There are eight million people in New York. They go there for many different reasons. Going there to kill their wife is just not very high on the list of probabilities."

"We're not talking probabilities. We're talking this one particular situation. We can't reach the guy. He hasn't gotten back to us. Why not? What if it's because he's too busy tracking down his wife so he can kill her?"

Not seeming unduly concerned, Meg said, "Well, that's less bad than someone coming here and pushing us into chairs and doing the whole bit with the duct tape."

"I haven't ruled that out either," said Peter. "Believe me I haven't."

Meg was doing jumping jacks now. The water seemed viscous as she leaped and subsided; thick, slow-motion droplets flew from her arms and torso. Just slightly short of breath, she said, "Look, his going to New York probably has nothing even to do with his wife. And if it *is* about the wife, maybe it's something good. Maybe he's trying to woo her back, have a rapprochement."

Peter crossed his arms in satisfaction as he crushed that cheerful assessment. "Very romantic. But then what about the message on the coconut? That's just a coincidence?"

Meg had to admit that the message on the coconut was awkward. She moved on to high kicks as she tried to figure a way around it.

Peter went on in the meantime. "And here's what's worse," he said. "Oh shit, I just thought of this. This is really bad. What if he murders her in our apartment? What if that's his whole idea behind exchanging houses—so he has an anonymous place to do the deed? He lures her over there on some pretext or other—to talk about lawyers, talk about a settlement, whatever--and he bumps her off right there in our living room. Leaves her dead on the floor, maybe in that little alcove where the globe is. What then, huh? He takes off, no one even knew he was there, no one can trace his movements, and meanwhile we've got a corpse in our apartment stinking up the whole building. That's great. That's just great."

Meg said, "I strongly doubt we have a corpse in our apartment. Try to relax. Why not get in the pool. It's heated. Perfect temperature."

"Right," he said. "Get in the pool. La-di-da, we're the obvious suspects in a murder case, let's go for a swim. Let's just backstroke all the way to the electric chair."

"Honey, there is no murder case. There's no murder case, no duct tape, and no corpse. And even if there was a corpse, we wouldn't be suspects. We're here, we have an alibi. And there isn't any motive."

"So now you're admitting that maybe there *is* a body in our living room."

"I'm not admitting any such thing. Listen, I have an idea. How about a back rub? Take your shirt off, lie down on a lounge. I'll rub your back. Nice and slow. It'll help you calm down."

"Naked?"

"No, just take your shirt off."

"No, I mean you. You're going to give me a back rub naked? Right out here in the open like this?"

"No one can see in."

Peter hesitated. Then he sighed, as though he'd be taking a big chance by letting his mind move away even for a moment from the problem at hand. But finally he took his shirt off and lay down on his stomach. The first feel of the air against his skin and the rays of the sun penetrating through it came as a genuine and profound surprise to him. Halfway through a New York winter he'd almost forgotten what those things felt like. The air, even as warm as it was, slightly tickled as it licked along his neck. The sunshine instantly coaxed open his constricted pores and drew forth a faint and sensuous film of perspiration, a kind of perpetual basting.

Meg unceremoniously straddled his backside and started working on the knotted muscles of his shoulders. It soon became clear that they weren't going to release without a fight. She urged him in whispers to let his mind slow down, focus on the breath.

He tried. He really tried. It was truly difficult, and trying that hard only made it more so. But for Peter, being tightly wound wasn't just a fleeting state but a defining habit, a stance toward life, a philosophy of nervous tension. And philosophies are probably not alterable by massage.

Still, caringly, patiently, Meg worked on his stubborn shoulders, his neck, his spine. Now and then she managed to get a coo or at least a grunt of pleasure out of him, and when her fingertips told her that she had finally made some progress, she let her torso fold forward against her husband's back and she nibbled on his ear. "Now I have another idea," she purred. "Let's make love."

That made Peter twitch. "Here? Now?"

"Here and now is where we are. Come on, we're in Key West, let's misbehave a little."

She said this with a charmingly youthful what-the-hell giggle that not even her husband could resist and he turned over as she was smoothly rolling off of him. They were working together to get his belt undone when there was a knock on the front door. It was a jaunty, cheerful knock, and plenty firm enough to be heard out by the pool.

"Oh shit," said Meg, as she scrambled to her feet and scampered around to find her cover-up, "that must be the glass man."

"Glass man?"

"I called him up between yoga and the pool. Can't just sit here with a broken window, can we?"

5.

"Hm," said the glass man, thoughtfully examining what was left of the smashed window. "Hit from the outside."

"Isn't that how windows usually get broken?" Peter said.

"That's about what you'd think, idn't it?" said the glass man, whose name was Freddy. He was tall and skinny, with high and stiff black hair that seemed to have been blown into a permanent off-center upsweep by the salt wind coming through the always open window of his truck. "I mean, that'd be the usual way. Busted from the outside in. But that don't hold in what might be called domestic situations."

"You see a lot of those?" asked Meg.

"Down here, hell yeah. Couples get liquored up, drugged out, next thing you know there's a small misunderstanding and a mango or a six-pack or a fry pan gets heaved through a window. Yup, happens."

He broke off to scratch a bug bite and Peter tried without success to place his accent. The reason he couldn't place it is because Freddy was a seventh-generation Key Wester, one of the thinning breed of true Conchs, and the Conch accent is not quite like any other. It rises here and there with a bit of Cuban lilt, then gets flattened out again with a layer of Southern drawl, which is spiked in turn by certain acidic vowel sounds that are seldom heard south of Boston.

"Yup, happens," Freddy said again, warming to his subject. "Weird stuff sometimes. Like one time a couple years ago I had a repair that ended up in court. Two ladies fighting over a dildo. Excuse my language, but that's what it was, a dildo. Fancy model. Lit up or something. Spun around I think. Ended up as evidence. I had to identify it 'cause I'd seen it laying there in a pool of glass. That bad boy had some heft to him. Anyway, never know what you're gonna find when you're on a mission for Guzman Glass."

"Guzman Glass?" said Peter. "That's your company?"

"*My* company?" said Freddy, with a quick self-deprecating laugh. "No, I just work for it. Owner's Carlos Guzman. You've never heard of Carlos Guzman?"

Meg and Peter admitted that they hadn't.

"You spend much time down here, you will. He's one of the big dogs. Owns a bunch of businesses, a lot of real estate. Some people think he owns the cops and city council too, but that's not anything you'd ever hear me say."

He broke off with a knowing wink then looked more widely around the living room at the off-white-upholstered wicker furniture, the tasteful lamps, the coffee table strewn with glossy magazines. "This is a damn nice house," he went on. "I've always liked this house."

"So you've been here before?"

Freddy didn't quite smother a chuckle. "Oh sure, number of times. I mean, Benny and Glenda, you know how they are."

"Actually, we don't," said Peter. "We're just down here on a home exchange."

"Ah, I figured you were friends. Guess I oughta keep my big mouth shut."

"Why?" asked Meg. "We're curious about them. Just normal human curiosity. What are they like?"

Freddy briefly weighed discretion against the joys of chitchat and discretion didn't have a chance. "They're a trip," he said. "Mutt and Jeff. Glenda, she's about six feet tall. Or maybe she just looks that way in those big high shoes she wears, the kind, you know, that make women wobble when they walk. Big hair, big face, big lipstick. Benny, he's maybe five foot five, bald on top, not fat but round, powerful, you know, built like the kid no one could tackle in a football game, you went to hit him and just bounced off. They both talk pretty loud, the way New Yorkers do. Guess they need to be heard over the traffic or the subway or something. Anyway, they're funny, friendly. I come to fix a window, right away they offer me a glass of wine, some cold cuts. Smiling, laughing, couldn't be nicer. A week later there's another window. Benny pays me in cash. Never writes a check, never asks for a bill. Takes out a wad of money and pays me. He's old school, he's a throwback."

Meg and Peter took that in. It was odd to be learning about people while standing in their living room, surrounded by their furniture, their knickknacks, as if their home were some sort of elaborate museum diorama. All that was missing were the informational placards: *This was their habitat; note the sophisticated remote controls for the wireless entertainment unit. This whimsical rabbit-eared corkscrew and chrome-plated cocktail strainer were among the tools they used.*

Feeling that he should repay some of Freddy's information, Peter said, "Well, there might be fewer broken windows from now on. I've heard they're separated, maybe getting divorced."

"Really? Wow. I didn't know Mafia got divorced."

Meg said, "Excuse me?"

"You know, there's the Catholic thing. And the honor thing. And the family thing. I mean, I guess these guys have girlfriends on the side, they're hardly home, but you never hear about 'em getting divorced, do you?"

Peter's shoulders had knotted up again. "Wait a second, let's back up a step. We're not talking about the social mores of Italian Catholics. We're talking about the guy whose house we're living in. He's Mafia?"

Freddy shrugged, ran a hand through his upswept hair, backpedaled a bit. "Hey, that's just the rumor among us working guys. What do we know? Mainly it's just that he pays everybody cash. Maybe he just doesn't like banks. Who does? Anyway, it's probably bulldinky, just another local legend. Forget you ever heard it."

He broke off, seemed to remember something, then started peering around the room at the level of the floor moldings. "You babysitting the cat?"

"Cat?" said Meg. "No, there's no cat."

"No way we could babysit a cat," Peter added. "I'm really allergic."

"Guess Benny took the cat with him," Freddy mulled.

"To our apartment?" Peter said. He suddenly sneezed at the mere idea of it. The thought of a cat in their apartment was almost as bad as the thought of a corpse in the little alcove where the globe was. He'd get asthma. He'd get hives. He'd itch so bad that his wrists and ankles would bleed from the scratching. "No, our listing specifically says no cats allowed."

"Me, I usually don't like 'em either," Freddy said. "This is a pretty cool cat, though. Fancy. Burmese, I think. Yellow eyes. Won't drink water from a bowl, only from a faucet. You have to get the drip just right or it shows you its ass and walks away. One time I came over, I was kind of high, I admit it, and I just watched the cat drink water from the faucet, the way it timed the drops. Forgot all about the stupid window. But all right, lemme get to work. I'll see if I've got the right size on the truck."

Meg said, "You want a deposit or a credit card or anything?"

"Nah," said Freddy. "Benny'll pay me whenever he gets back. Benny's good for it."

6.

"I can't believe he brought a cat," said Peter. "Brought a cat to our apartment."

They were sitting at a fish joint over on Caroline Street, a place called JB's Grouper Wagon. The establishment had started, some decades earlier, literally as a wagon, a portable kitchenette that the original JB, a hulking fellow with an extravagant red beard, had pushed around on shaky wheels salvaged from a shopping cart. He'd had an ice box, a deep-fat fryer, an aluminum pan piled with a subsiding mound of shredded lettuce, some slabs of doughy Cuban bread and three or four bottles of hot sauce; that was it, except for the stacks of grouper filets straight off the boats. Like most places in Key West, JB's had gotten gentrified in recent years. But gentrification is relative, and in this case what started as a wagon had now become a shack. It had a roof but no walls. There was a counter where you put your order in and a kitchen behind a flimsy divider. Archaic license plates, mostly from the southern states, were nailed up here and there on posts. There was a rail at barstool height that paralleled the sidewalk and a few picnic-style slatted tables. The lunch rush had died down by the time Meg and Peter had arrived and they'd been able to score one of those.

Meg pulled some paper napkins out of the dispenser and tried to wipe a blob of dried ketchup off the table. "We don't know that he brought the cat," she said. "There are a lot of other places the cat could be. The cat could be in a cat hotel. The cat could be at a friend's house. Or maybe the wife, this Glenda, ended up with the cat. I think that's a lot more likely. A breakup, the wife usually gets the pet, the kids. That's how it usually works, right?"

Peter stuck with his own line of thought. "The listing very clearly says no cats. Small, short-haired dogs okay. Children, inquire. No cats permitted. Owner allergic. That's clearly what it says. If he brought a cat, I'm filing a complaint. I'm putting it in feedback."

Meg said, "That'll show him. I'm starving. You?"

Peter in fact was too worried to be hungry, but he'd ordered a fish sandwich with rice and beans because he was afraid that if he didn't he'd start losing weight.

His wife said, "Think I'm going to have a beer. You?"

Peter nodded absently and Meg went back up to the counter. By the time she came back with two Coronas Peter had added another item to his portfolio of dread. "Shit," he said, "you know what I think? I think he's using the cat as bait."

"Bait?"

"To lure the wife to the apartment. Look, it makes perfect sense. He knows she's in New York. He knows she loves the cat. He calls her up, says you want to see the cat, come to 680 West End Avenue, apartment 5J. She shows up all happy with a ball of yarn or a velvet mouse or whatever people bring a cat, bends over to pet it, and he knifes her in the back. Bye-bye Glenda. He slips out, and now we've got not just a dead body in our apartment but an orphaned cat, too. That's great. That's just great."

A waitress brought the sandwiches. They were piled high with lettuce, tomato and onions. Meg squashed hers down to a manageable thickness and a squib of aioli trickled out the side. This was a new wrinkle. The original JB would never have heard of aioli.

Washing down the first bite with some beer, she said, "You know what I think is kind of funny?"

"Funny? I don't think any of it's funny. I think we're in big, big trouble."

"What I think is kind of funny is that you're more concerned about the cat than about the fact that the guy might be a Mafioso."

"Hey, I'm concerned about that too," said Peter, a little bit defensively, as if he'd been remiss in some aspect of his worrying. "I'm concerned about that plenty."

"Too many onions on this sandwich," said Meg, tugging a few translucent rings out from the mix. "Anyway, it's probably just a rumor."

"Or not. Little bald tough guy with a big showy wife. Hot temper. Wads of cash. I mean, if the shoe fits—"

"We don't know he's a tough guy. He's got a Burmese cat. How tough can he be?"

"Killers often have a soft spot for animals. Look at what's his name, the Birdman of Alcatraz."

"That was a movie," Meg said.

"Based on a true story," Peter insisted. "But okay, leave that on the side for now. Look at everything else about the guy. Big house in Key West. How's he pay for it? Does he have a job? I doubt it. Guys with jobs can't just pick up and go to New York on a whim. This guy went last minute, right?"

"So did we," Meg pointed out. "Maybe the guy's a literature professor."

"Ha. Have you seen one single book in the house?"

"Yes, as a matter of fact I have. *Fifty Shades.* On a shelf on the wife's side nightstand."

"Great. They break some windows then they spank each other."

"All I'm saying is that you can't jump to conclusions about people. I mean, a little detail here and there and you assume the guy is some bigshot Mafio—"

She did not complete the word because at that instant she heard a gravelly voice behind her say, "'Scuse me, ma'am."

Wheeling toward the soft but quietly insistent sound, she saw a very old man with a chihuahua on his lap and a fish sandwich on the table in front of him. The old man had an enormous fleshy nose and a lavish head of white hair tinged slightly yellow at the ends. He had a large and mobile mouth, black eyes set deep in papery-looking sockets, and he was wearing a turquoise linen shirt with navy blue piping and a monogram on the left chest pocket.

"I couldn't help overhearing your conversation," the old man went on, "and while I personally am in no way not to any degree bothered or disturbed by it, I thought it might be a good thing if I mentioned that there might conceivably be other people who could take, um, let's call it umbrage or offense at having certain things talked about so publicly in such a, well, let's say public tone of voice, and so, just in the hope that maybe I could spare you any possible whaddyacallit, any unpleasantness or discomfort while you're on vacation, I wanted to suggest in a very friendly way that maybe you should talk a little softer. That's all I have to say. 'Scuse me for butting in."

Peter studied the old man as he spoke—studied him through the lens of his ready paranoia—and quickly concluded beyond a reasonable doubt that he was Mafia too. The big collar and top-stitching on his shirt; the elevated rambling that failed to mask what was clearly an Outer Borough accent. Christ, was everybody Mafia in this town? Where the hell had they landed? Camden, New Jersey? Providence, Rhode Island? Feeling it would be prudent to show respect, Peter began fumbling for an apology.

The old man peaceably lifted a wrinkled and long-fingered hand. "Hey, nothing to be sorry for. Like I said, I didn't take one iota of offense. Taking offense about every little thing, it's a waste of time and energy, and let's face it, I don't have that much of either. Anyway, my name's Bert. This here is Nacho. He's whaddyacallit, hyper-allergenic, he won't bother your allergies."

"You heard that too?" said Peter. "About the allergies?"

"Still got pretty good hearing. Say hello, Nacho." He gently took the chihuahua's tiny paw and made the dog wave it. The dog, apparently tired of the waving routine that was repeated each and every time its master made some new acquaintance, yawned widely then snorted. "Anyway," Bert said, "nice to meet you both."

The three of them shared benign though not exactly natural smiles and then Bert began to swivel slowly back toward his own table. Halfway turned, he said, "But 'scuse me, this individual you were speaking of, the one with the cat and the wad of cash and the wife toward whom he might or might not possibly harbor some ill-feeling and violent intentions, I'm curious. Would you like to tell me what this individual's name might be?"

Meg and Peter took a brief meeting with their eyes, then Meg said in a newly cautious undertone, "Benny Bufano."

"Ah." Bert's face was as unreadable as Hungarian.

"You know him?" Peter asked.

Bert elected not to answer that. Continuing his slow swivel, he said, "Me and Nacho, we're here most days. Lemme know if I can do anything for you. I'll leave you to finish your lunch. *Buon appetito.*"

Part 2

7.

One hundred and ten miles away by water, twice as far by road, in a very different sort of outpost on the Gulf of Mexico, Glenda Fortuna Bufano was giving herself a pedicure and saying, "Jesus Christ, it's dull around here."

She had not so far been murdered by her husband, certainly not in the Kaplans' apartment in the little alcove where the globe was. She was a thousand miles from New York, though it's true that she had fled there a month or so before when she'd stormed out on Benny, or rather when she'd wobbled out on platform shoes that made her ankles hurt. But New York in winter hadn't worked for her; no place would have worked for her, given her confused and miserable state of mind; and after a few weeks of gray skies, festering resentments, and gnawing regrets, she'd bolted again, this time to her father's grand estate in Florida. Now, still in a mood somewhere between a snit and a funk, she was working on her toenails while gazing past the lip of the cobalt-tiled infinity pool, across the faultless lawn and beyond the dunes dotted with sea oats to the flat green expanse of the Gulf.

"It isn't dull," her father disagreed. "It's peaceful and quiet and safe. What's wrong with a little peace and quiet?"

"Nothing. When you're dead."

The father gave his leonine head an amused and indulgent shake. He was an almost handsome man, with flinty eyes, a chin with a hint of a cleft, and a broad nose with a slightly flattened bridge. "Ah, Glenda. My baby. So much like your late mother. Always bitching."

The daughter seemed to take this as encouragement. Her wide dark eyes flashed, her carefully shaped eyebrows lifted into a steeper arc, her broad wry mouth curled in vigorous complaint. "And the Italian food down here," she went on. "How can they even call it Italian? Where's the rosemary? Where's the garlic? Where's the taste? Calling it Italian food, that should be illegal. Maybe I should've stayed in Manhattan. Cold as hell but at least you can get a decent piece of bread. And why the hell do they call this cemetery Naples anyway? You know what they should call it? They should call it Michigan. They should call it fucking Ohio. Fucking Canada."

Glenda's dad, Ralph "the Fortune" Fortuna, tried to muster a tone of disapproval, but that was something he'd never quite been able to pull off in regard to his beloved only child. "That language, Glenda. Where did you pick up that language?"

"Where? How about around the dinner table, where you used to bring home all those wavy-haired goombahs, one of which, with your blessing as I recall, became my asshole of a husband."

Almost nostalgically, Fortuna said, "Benny *did* have wavy hair back then, didn't he?" Then he raised a finger and went on with something approaching sternness. "But that was a long time ago. Things were different then. I was different then. Very different."

This was something Ralph Fortuna badly wanted to believe. He'd come up from the street, and though he claimed as people always did that he was not ashamed of that, he certainly didn't advertise it either. He'd started his career in Staten Island as a low-level Mob associate who, by virtue of his loyalty and zeal, was soon promoted to made man. He'd profited from the traditional rackets--gambling, extortion, finagling no-show jobs--and within a few years, by a standout combination of ruthlessness and cunning, was out-earning nearly all of his contemporaries. He had his own crew by thirty-five and was quite a rich man by forty. At that point he decided it was beneath his dignity to get his own hands dirty, and that's where it all got sort of hazy.

Fortuna, in recent years thought of rather vaguely as a businessman/investor, had never for a moment stopped being a criminal; but he'd become far subtler about it and he wanted to believe that the really messy and brutish parts of his career had been the work of an entirely different person. This brash, crude, violent Ralphie Fortune—who could he possibly have been? Certainly not the well-tanned and conservatively dressed gentleman who played golf at charity events with the elite of Naples, who owned a waterfront mansion with ten guest suites and a dozen marble bathrooms, and who for years had secretly hired tutors to improve his diction.

Coming back to the subject of her estranged husband's hair loss, Glenda said, "He blames me that most of it fell out. Says I drove him crazy, made it fall out in clumps from aggravation. Good. I hope I did. I hope the rest of it falls out in the bathtub. Now let's not talk about

Benny anymore. He makes me sick."

She leaned far forward in her lounge chair and with quiet fury got back to the task of removing chipped old polish from her toenails with a cotton ball. The laboratory smell of acetone mixed uneasily with the salt air and the muskiness of sun-baked palms. Her father said, "Why do you still bother doing that yourself? Why not treat yourself to a nice spa day? Take the Maserati, go up to the Ritz. Get a massage, a facial, let them do the pedicure."

She looked up as if the generous suggestion had for some reason made her angry. "I don't want somebody else to the pedicure, okay? I don't feel like having some tiny Asian person messing with my feet."

"What do you have against Asians?"

"Nothing whatsoever. I wish all twenty billion of them long and happy lives. I just don't feel like having some stranger fucking around with my toes, okay?"

Ralph Fortuna allowed himself a silent sigh and went back to reading his *Wall Street Journal.* Glenda was in one of her moods, and when she was like that, you just couldn't talk to her. He'd learned that long before, but still, it was frustrating. The odd thing was that Glenda also realized she was being childish and impossible; she knew it, and she couldn't stop. Why? She didn't act this way with anyone else. With other people she was reasonable and agreeable and charming. With other people she behaved like an adult. But when it came to dealing with her father—and, okay, sometimes her husband—that grown-up stuff went out the window. It was one of those things she just didn't understand.

There were plenty of things about Glenda that her father didn't understand either. Why did she still insist on cursing so much, talking as if she'd never left the street? Why couldn't she accept the facts of being comfortable, respectable? Pondering the mystery of family and not quite knowing that he was about to speak aloud, Fortuna said, "Maybe I shouldn't have let you marry Benny."

"Ha! Like you could have stopped me."

"No. But I could have stopped him."

Looking up abruptly from her toenails, Glenda said, "So why didn't you?" She said this in her usual flippant tone but along with the edge there was genuine curiosity in the simple question.

"Because I thought it was what you wanted. I wanted you to be happy."

Both father and daughter wanted to believe this but neither one quite could. True, Glenda, at twenty-one, had been head over heels with Benny. He was funny and attentive and had a roosterish swagger that she found both sexy and endearingly absurd. Still, it had been her father who'd brought them together, and it was her father's purposes that were best served by having them marry. A daughter who would always be close by; a son-in-law he basically owned; in all, a somewhat medieval but handy arrangement.

"Well," said Glenda, "it hasn't quite worked out, has it?"

"There've been good years," her father said.

There was no way in hell that Glenda was going to acknowledge that just then. She maintained a sulky silence as she tossed aside the cotton ball and moved on to applying fresh polish in a purplish shade of red. She did one toenail, two, and the silence stretched on. The breeze was still and nothing moved in the perfect yard. Tiny wavelets died at the edge of the Gulf but made no sound. The quiet was somehow cumulative, it took on a weird and empty momentum, and at some point, inevitably, it brought Glenda back to her previous complaint. "I'm bored stiff around here! This sitting around a mansion all day, I just don't get it. You got freakin' mansions all around you and nobody's home. Nobody comes out. Nobody uses the beach. What is there, a fucking plague or something? I wish Tasha was here, at least."

"Tasha?" said her father. "Who's Tasha?"

"The cat. I miss her something awful."

A confused or perhaps pained expression flicked across Frank Fortuna's face before he could erase it. "I thought you didn't like the cat. I thought it was Benny's cat."

"It was. It is. And I didn't used to like her at all. Thought she was a stuck-up bitch. But she wore me down, what can I say? That way she purrs, you feel it all through her ribs. Now I miss her like crazy."

Her father said nothing and Glenda bided her time. She really thought he would offer to intervene—intervene as in getting hold of Benny and telling him to give her the cat. He'd occasionally done that sort of thing before. Not that it was what you'd call a healthy family dynamic: The father bossing around the husband, who in turn tried to boss around the wife, who in turn had her ways, generally but not always passive, of getting back at both of them. But this time Fortuna made no move toward getting involved. He went back to his *Journal* and she went back to her pedicure.

But at some point her hand began to tremble and she made a clumsy swipe with the brush that put a slash of polish on the knuckle of a toe. "Shit," she said. "God fucking damn it. This is stupid." With an unsteady hand she capped the polish bottle and for a moment she silently sat there contemplating her mismatched toenails. "It isn't just this boring town," she went on at last. "And it isn't just the cat I miss. I miss Benny. It's stupid, I know it is, but I really, really miss him. I want my husband back."

8.

Benny Bufano, who had no idea that his wife was missing him and no great faith that she ever wanted to see him again, was at that moment sitting at the Oyster Bar in New York's Grand Central Terminal, mostly ignoring the mixed dozen of Blue Points, Malpeagues, and Cotuits in front of him and drawing on a napkin.

His lunch companion, Mikey Ferraro, had known Benny a long time and was so accustomed to his constant doodling that he barely noticed it anymore. Long on appetite and short on empathy, neither did he notice that Benny, even with a beautiful plate of oysters in front of him, did not seem happy. In fact Benny was miserable. He didn't want to be in New York. He especially didn't want to be in New York on a job. Most of all, he didn't want to be in New York on the particular job for which he'd been summoned. The thought of that job made him queasy, and the queasiness in turn made his plate of oysters seem unappetizing in the extreme.

Mikey, a giant of a man whose pearl gray suit jacket was stretched tight across his massive back and whose skin was tinged a strange coppery orange from cosmetic attempts at a sunless tan, slurped a Malpeague and mopped his flubbery lips on a napkin. "Here's what I don't get," he said. "The oysters here, they're the same fuckin' oysters you get all over town. I mean, these people, you think they have slobs all up and down the coast digging oysters just for them? Same fuckin' oysters, trust me. But they taste better here, don't they?"

Benny forced himself to choke down a Cotuit but said nothing.

Mikey gulped several more before speaking again. "You like one kind better than the others? For me, Blue Points are still the Cadillac."

Benny just shrugged but his face was not designed for hiding his emotions. He had slightly bulging and emphatic eyes whose whites stood out against his suntanned olive skin and that brightened or dimmed with his mood. His wide mouth gave him a hint of dimples when he smiled and thickened his chin when he frowned. As his hairline had receded, it could be seen that his scalp took on a mottled flush when he was upset, and even Mikey eventually noticed that he was upset now.

The big man put both hands on the counter in front of him and leaned close enough to Benny so that Benny could smell the stuff he used to stiffen up his hair. "Listen, I know you're ticked off at me, but let's try to be professional at least. You think I got a choice here? You think I get to pick my spots any more'n you do? You know how the Big Guy does things. It's your turn in the batting order, you get the job."

Quietly but firmly, Benny said, "Nobody should have to do this job. This job should not be done. It ain't right."

Mikey had picked up another oyster. He put it down again. "Right? Since when are things right? Listen, I got some advice for you. Quit bellyachin', do the fuckin' job, get it over with. Then get drunk, get laid, and forget it ever happened."

Benny kept sulking and drawing and Mikey went back to his lunch. But the fact that his companion seemed to have no appetite finally began to interfere with his own enjoyment of the food, and this he found infuriating. Suddenly, sort of retroactively, his patience was used up and he was very annoyed at Benny. Gesturing with the absurdly small oyster fork that was clutched in his enormous hand, he said, "Will you please quit the fuckin' doodling and eat? And another thing. You're not doing yourself any favors being such a pain in the ass about this, having to be dragged up here, having to get the Big Guy's Miami crew involved..."

Benny didn't like the sound of that at all. "The Miami crew? Why the Miami crew?"

"Why? Because the Big Guy got tired of your stalling and pissing and moaning so he had some Miami nobody drive all the way down the Keys to deliver a message to your house."

"To my house? But I'm here already!"

Mikey shrugged. "Guess the guy didn't get the memo. Plus, it was unfortunate that the window that the message went through wasn't open at the time."

"He broke my window? That's bullshit. Listen, I got innocent people staying at my house."

"Maybe you shoulda thought of that before you stalled so fucking long."

Mikey went back to his oysters. But the chill was off them and they didn't taste as good as they had before. Melted ice sloshed as he pushed the platter away from him and he continued to blame the spoiled lunch on Benny. "You're making problems, man. Think about it. The Big Guy's got a dozen crew he's trying to keep happy. He can't give special treatment to one guy just 'cause he's the son-in-law. He does that, he's got eleven pissed off guys. And who are they gonna be pissed at? You, if you keep acting like some prima donna twat."

For a moment Benny said nothing. The room around them hummed with conversation and crackled with the sharp snap of crab legs being broken. Finally, more with sadness than anger, Benny put down his pencil and said, "We used to be pretty good friends, Mikey. I find that kind of amazing now."

The mildness of the answer made Mikey realize he'd gone too far. "Look," he said, "it's a shit job, I admit it. I wouldn't be too damn happy to do it either."

He paused, hoping Benny would meet him halfway in his attempt at conciliation. Benny didn't. He was nursing a grievance that could not be halfway mollified, and Mikey finally broke down and addressed it.

"Okay," he went on. "Can we talk? About the cat? I know you're upset about the cat. I don't blame you. The thing with the cat, that was harsh. But it wasn't my idea."

Suddenly feisty, Benny said, "I don't care whose idea it was. Why'd you have to—"

Mikey cut him off with a quick raise of a hand and a lift of an eyebrow and a fast and surreptitious glance toward the entrance of the restaurant. A woman had just walked in. There was nothing at all remarkable about her appearance; she looked a lot like the tens of thousands of other women who milled around midtown on business days. Her hair was brown, just a shade richer than could be called mousy, gathered up at the back of her head so you couldn't really tell how long it was. Her face was neither more nor less than pleasant, her makeup tastefully but not expertly applied. Beneath a presentable though not stylish cloth coat, she seemed to have an average figure, which is to say she always imagined she would look better if she could drop that last five pounds. She wore appropriate mid-heel shoes whose clicking echoed softly beneath the low vaulted ceiling of the restaurant. Without hesitation she strolled over to the main counter and took a seat that was being saved for her by a man in a navy blue suit.

"That's her," Mikey said simply. "Lydia Greenspan. She's here most days around this time. The suit, that's her contact. Him we still need. Him we leave alone."

Benny felt sick as he watched the marked woman. His vision blurred at the edges and there was a ringing somewhere deep in his skull. From where he sat, he saw the woman mostly in profile. She had a slightly upturned nose; her ear was small, pegged with a simple pearl earring. He didn't want to kill her. He didn't want to kill anyone, certainly not a woman. Killing people was in fact a blank line on his resume. By luck or maybe by a carefully veiled nepotism, he'd always been spared those jobs before. No longer. He watched as the woman shook hands with the man sitting next to her. They shared what appeared to be a bit of casual, collegial conversation and then the man pulled out his phone. He brought up an image, showed it to her, and the two of them laughed.

"See," whispered Mikey, "the laugh, that's part of the ruse. Like he's showing her a selfie or a picture of his dog or something. He isn't. He's passing her the information."

The man in the blue suit put the phone away. The target woman stopped laughing and brushed some loose strands of hair back from her forehead.

"Now she'll sit a couple minutes," Mikey went on, "then slip off to the ladies' room and write the tip down on a little scrap of paper. She'll come back, eat a little something, then she goes upstairs and meets the other contact under the big clock. She passes off the scrap of paper, leaves the building on the Vanderbilt Avenue side, and grabs a taxi up to the West Side, 93rd Street, where she lives. That's probably your best chance to nail her, when she's going home. Got it?"

Benny said nothing. He was staring blankly at the woman's cloth coat and the bundle of hair at the back of her head. He wished she didn't look so ordinary, just like somebody's sister or somebody ahead of you in the supermarket line.

"So it's your gig now," said Mikey. "Scope it out, handle it your way. But don't wait too long. Your cat's looking awfully skinny."

"You're not feeding her, you son of a bitch?"

"Bad enough I had to drive all the way to Florida to kidnap the fucking thing. Buying cat food's where I draw the line. Good luck, Benny."

9.

In Key West it had been such a perfect afternoon and evening that Peter Kaplan had at moments nearly forgotten to be worried.

After lunch he and Meg had rented bicycles for their expected though by no means certain two week stay and had ridden them at a sightseeing pace along the broad promenade that flanked the ocean. Coasting pelicans had tracked their progress; young couples riding tandem on laboring motor scooters had honked and waved; even the grizzled men who loitered on the seawall in shredded jeans and faded bandanas, nipping at cheap booze, looked up and smiled as they passed. The sun shone, the palms swayed, the whole town seemed entirely benign if slightly goofy; how could anything really bad possibly happen here?

Sunset and dinner took Peter's tentative foray into the carefree to a yet higher level. Watching from the end of White Street Pier, he and Meg had held hands as the orange sun first skimmed the horizon then seemed not so much to sink as to melt into the sea, leaving behind a spreading sheen that went from pink to lavender to indigo. Dinner was at a beachside restaurant called Casa Carlos and was accompanied by a more than acceptable bottle of wine and a rather decadent shared dessert that proved to be the perfect prelude to the lovemaking that had been so inconveniently squelched earlier in the day.

In all, it had been a splendid few hours of vacationing, and by the time Peter had flossed his teeth, checked his scalp for hair loss and his face for possible basal cells, and nestled into bed with his wife, who was already sleeping, serenely and profoundly, as she always did, his attitude had been quite thoroughly if provisionally adjusted. Home exchanging, he thought; it was supposed to be an adventure, right? You never knew exactly what you'd find, what might happen. That was part of the fun. A broken window; a flying coconut; a host with Mafia connections: Why not try a little harder to chill out and accept those oddities and mishaps? Why not embrace them? They were the stuff of vivid memories and amusing stories to share with friends back home.

This new and easygoing frame of mind lulled Peter into a delicious slumber that lasted until around one a.m., when he was awakened by what seemed to him to be a noise downstairs.

It wasn't a loud noise. In fact he wasn't quite sure he'd heard anything at all. But something must have registered because he felt a small squirt of adrenaline that rendered him instantly alert. What he thought he'd heard was a metallic sound that was crisper and dryer than the humidly rustling sounds of tropical night. The sound might perhaps have been the tiny collision of a key or a pick with a lock, the rubbing ca-chunk of a deadbolt sliding in its groove. The sound was followed by something less heard than very faintly felt—the subtle whoosh that happened when a door was opened and a whole house exhaled through a vacant frame.

Peter lifted onto an elbow and cupped an ear to listen. His heart had begun to race a bit and to feel a little bit confined inside his chest, but he wasn't yet in full-on emergency mode. He didn't want to panic, didn't want to backslide into automatic worry. Most night sounds, after all, were innocent and harmless, even comforting—fronds scratching, small shy creatures on the move in darkness, houses sighing and porches settling as they shed the heat of day. Probably he'd heard nothing but sounds like those. His heart rate slowed again and he began to lower his head back toward the pillow.

That was when he heard a soft but rhythmic sequence—shuffle, creak; shuffle, creak—that he felt could only be footsteps in the living room below. The quiet but insistent beat came three times, four times, and as the pictured footsteps drew nearer, all trace of calm was swept out of Peter's mind by a flooding tide of sickening fear made even more bitter by a jolt of self-mockery and self-blame: A benign, safe little town—ha! This was what happened when you relented in your paranoia, when you relaxed your vigilance even for a moment. He reached over and shook Meg by the shoulder.

Her response was just a sleepy, "Hm?"

He shook her again then brought his face very close to hers and said in a choked whisper, "Wake up. There's someone in the house."

His tone jarred her into full alertness and for a moment they just sat together in the dark, a tangled sheet around their legs, listening and dreading.

From below there came more sounds: Objects being bumped,

something being placed on a tabletop or counter.

Peter whispered, "It's the guy who broke the window, made the threats. Shit. We shouldn't have stayed here. I knew we shouldn't have. We should've bolted. He's here to kill someone."

Meg's only answer was to tug her husband's arm so that he followed her as she slid silently onto the floor at the side of the bed that was farthest from the bedroom door. The two of them cowered there behind the mattress, kneeling like children at their prayers. Peter fought back a shameful impulse to weep. Somewhere deep in the dark center of his lifelong nervousness there had always been a certainty that a moment like this would come—a moment of crisis to which he would not be equal, a moment when he would miserably fail to meet a danger and therefore be destroyed. Well, goddamn it, destroyed he might be—tied up with duct tape, shot by mistake—but he wouldn't quail and he wouldn't go down without a fight.

Footsteps began ascending the unlighted stairway from the living room.

Meg kissed her husband on the cheek. She whispered, "Whatever happens, Peter, I love you."

"I love you too," he said, and as he said the simple words he also formed a stratagem. There was a small lamp on the nightstand. He disconnected it and grabbed it with a sweating hand. Something to throw.

The footsteps continued, coming closer. Outside, palms rustled, toads bleated, crickets rasped. The noises blended, seeming to become infernally loud, amplified by the rush of blood coursing deep inside Meg's and Peter's ears.

The footsteps paused; the intruder must have reached the landing.

Peter tried to shout; he couldn't. It was like that moment in a nightmare when you try to scream but nothing happens. He begged his throat to open, and finally, in a tone he wished was more authoritative, he managed to call out, "Stop! Don't come any closer. I have a gun."

There was a pause. The landing was dark. The bedroom was dark.

The silence seemed to quell the other night sounds and to last a long time.

Finally, emboldened by the sound of his own voice and by the fragile hope that his bluff was working, Peter went on. "And listen, you're wasting your time here. I'm not Benny Bufano and I don't know where he is."

Meg, nestled up against her husband's side, called out, "And I'm not Glenda."

There was another pause. This one somehow carried the suggestion of befuddlement, of a mythic riddle being pondered.

Then a voice from the landing said, "Fuckin' A, you're not Glenda. Because I am. So who the fuck are you?"

Without further hesitation Glenda strode into the bedroom on her platform shoes and switched on a light. In the sudden glare she saw that her bed was all messed up and that two naked strangers were kneeling on the floor with a sheet around their shoulders. Her glance eventually settled on Peter's right arm and she said rather dismissively, "You have a gun, huh? Bullshit, you have a gun. You have a lamp."

Peter had sort of forgotten he had the projectile in his hand. Sheepishly, he put it back on the nightstand.

Meg said to Glenda, "You don't have a gun either? Or duct tape?"

"Don't be ridiculous, Hon," said Glenda. "I live here. I'm looking for my cat. I'm looking for my husband. Maybe you two should put some clothes on and tell me what the fuck is going on."

10.

"Ladies and gentlemen," said the expert from D.C., addressing an early morning meeting of thirty or so FBI agents, most of whom didn't want to be there, "the most important thing I have to say to you today comes down to simply this: Forget everything you think you know about the Mob. Forget Don Corleone. Forget Tony Soprano. Forget quaint little crimes like protection rackets, gambling, arson. That was twentieth-century fun and games, and today's Mafia has moved light years beyond it. How does the Mob make its serious money today? I'll give it to you in three simple words: white collar crime. Embezzlement from major banks and brokerages that sometimes don't even know they've been robbed of tens of millions. Stock price manipulation and insider trading on an epic scale. Ponzi schemes, rogue hedge funds. That's where the money is, in the very heart of our financial system. So how does the Mob elbow in to that sphere? Not with baseball bats and handguns. No, the Mob infiltrates with financial expertise and tremendous sophistication in computer technology. Break-ins today don't happen in people's homes or place of business; they happen in our computer networks because of security flaws that are exploited by brilliant and amoral hackers in league with savvy but crooked bankers and brokers, who in turn do the bidding of thoroughly modern mobsters who are much smarter than we give them credit for. Today's Organized Crime— O.C.— has everything to do with I.T., and we ignore that at our peril..."

The expert from D.C. droned on for another forty minutes, and well before the end of his remarks Special Agent Andy Sheehan had given up on hiding his boredom. He shifted in his crummy metal chair, crossed and re-crossed his inconveniently long legs, and looked away from the speaker, past the cheap blinds on the frosty windows to an uninspiring cityscape in a blighted area of Queens. Sheehan hated being bored, hated it worse than anything except, perhaps, being told how to do his job. When he was bored, resentments sprouted, initially directed toward the person who was boring him but soon spreading wider. At that moment Sheehan's resentment was largely focused on the room he was sitting in and the office where he'd spent the past nineteen years of his working life. New York's Organized Crime division was an elite and much-decorated unit; why did the Bureau still hide them away in such a dump? The fluorescent lighting was hideous, chopped up into little squares by cheap fixtures that resembled ice-cube trays. The metal desks reminded him of the ones at the third-rate Catholic school where he'd attended grades K through twelve. And why did the brass keep sending up these mealy-mouthed bureaucrats to lecture career agents as though they were rookies?

When the talk finally ended, Andy grabbed Lou Duncan, one of the few guys on the squad he still really liked, and they went across the street to the Greek joint for a coffee. Stoic men and proud of it, they were the only people in the place who weren't wearing topcoats. They slid into a booth at the back and Duncan asked Sheehan what he'd thought of the presentation.

Predictably, Sheehan said it was total bullshit.

"Not total," Duncan disagreed. He was African-American, with skin that was almost more gray than brown and slightly pitted on his cheeks. He had a deep, soft, gravelly voice, a mild and unruffled manner, and a general approach to life and work that favored nuance over absolutes. "I mean," he went on, "can't disagree that the real money's in white-collar stuff."

"Sure, sure," said Sheehan, "but we didn't need some suit from Washington to tell us that. The part's that bullshit is saying that these guys we've been chasing all these years aren't knuckleheads anymore, that they've suddenly become rocket scientists because they know how to work an iPad."

Duncan sipped some coffee and said mildly, "They *are* smarter than they used to be. Relatively speaking."

"So this means we fight back with computers? Makes me sick," said Sheehan. "What does the Bureau fund these days? What's the recruiting about? What's the training about? Cyber-this and cyber-that. So we end up with wimps who think police work happens in front of a computer screen instead of on the street, who'd shit in their pants at the idea of going undercover—"

"Guys still do that," Duncan pointed out.

"Fewer and fewer. And hardly ever the young guys." This was a sore point with Sheehan, one of many when it came to recent changes at the Bureau. He'd always had a firm but brittle sense of how things should be done, and he'd never wavered in the conviction that his way was the right way. This unflagging certainty showed in everything about him. His posture was ramrod straight, with none of the shrinking or slouching one often saw in men who were six-foot four. The gaze from his pale blue eyes was direct but generally squeezed into a narrow beam, always looking for something fishy. His square chin jutted slightly as though he was daring someone to disagree with him. But for all his breathtaking confidence, even he had noticed lately that certain things were being done differently around the office, different things were being honored. It hurt him and drove him a little bit crazy that now, so close to the end of his career, his way of being a cop was no longer esteemed as the highest and the most effective way.

A waitress came over and sloshed more coffee in their cups. By the time she walked away Sheehan's tone had shifted from complaint to resolve. "But let me tell you something we both already know. The Mob is not run by computer. The Mob is run by guys who are still mostly knuckleheads. Have they figured a few things out? Of course. But by baby steps. Have they muscled in on new businesses? Sure. But they run them a lot like they ran the old businesses. This is what that schmuck expert doesn't understand. Even with the white collar stuff—"

Duncan slowed him down with a lift of a long-fingered hand. He said, "Wait a second. Why are you all wound up about this? I thought you weren't even working any white collar stuff."

"I'm not," said Sheehan. "Officially."

"Oh Christ, Andy. Don't tell me you're going cowboy again."

"Cowboy? No. Freelance, maybe."

"Shit. The last time you went freelance—"

"What? The last time I landed the Underboss of the Bonnano family."

"After almost getting killed. Almost getting suspended. Almost ending up in fucking jail."

"Yeah, but I didn't. And the job got done."

Duncan considered that, sipped some coffee. "Andy, how old are you now? Fifty?"

"Forty-nine."

"Like, eight months from a pension?"

"Six, but who's counting."

"Six months," said Duncan with his smooth, calm voice. "Most guys would be laying low, taking care of paperwork, running out the clock. You, you gotta go out with a bang or a thud."

Sheehan didn't bother trying to deny it. "I've made a little bet with myself," he said. "A hundred bucks. Want to get in on the action?"

"I don't gamble," said Lou Duncan. "You know that."

"Here's the bet. There's a guy in the office, Evan LeFroy—"

"Sure, I know Evan—"

"--A young brainy guy who thinks he can take down mobsters while sitting at his keyboard with his dick in one hand and a latte in the other. For months, all hush-hush, he's been tracking a crooked trader named Marc Orlovsky."

"If it's so hush-hush, how come you know about it?" Duncan asked.

By instinct Sheehan quickly scanned the luncheonette for eavesdroppers then leaned low across his coffee cup. "I know because I read his files."

Even the mild Duncan was exercised by this. "You read another agent's private files? Are you crazy?"

Sheehan did not address the question. Instead, he said, "Some computer maven. Big security and encryption expert. He goes out for long lunches and leaves his logged-on laptop right there on his desk."

"Guess he trusts his colleagues."

Sheehan let that pass. "So here's the story. This dirtbag Orlovsky has been making killer trades. Big trades. Consistently. Either he's got the world's best Ouija board or he's using insider information. Where's he getting it? Who's he working for? This wuss LeFroy thinks he can figure it out and get a big promotion while sitting at his desk and analyzing data. Fucking *data!* Fucking *graphs!* While sitting on his lazy ass. Can you believe that shit?"

"Yeah. I can. Totally."

"You're supposed to say you can't. Doesn't matter. Anyway, I'm taking a different approach."

"It's not your case," Duncan pointed out.

"A very basic approach," Sheehan said. "Law Enforcement 101. I've started tailing this Orlovsky."

"On your own? Without authorization?"

"Free country. I'm allowed to be curious. I'm allowed to walk behind somebody."

"Some people call that stalking."

"Only if it's badly done. But in the meantime I've got a bet to win. I've bet myself a hundred bucks I catch him first. If I win, I buy myself a first-rate steak dinner. If I lose, the money goes to Catholic Charities." He finished the last of his coffee then added, "You're the only who knows this, Lou."

"How'd I get so lucky?"

"Questions come up, where I am, what I'm doing, you'll cover for me, right?"

"Shit," said Duncan. "As far as I can. You know I will."

"Thanks. Might even share that steak with you."

"You haven't won it yet."

"I will," said Sheehan. "I will."

11.

Glenda had spent the night of her return to Key West as a guest in her own house.

Utterly drained by the long drive down from Naples, and by the crushing disappointment of not finding Benny at home in their long-shared bed, and by the bewilderment of discovering two quailing strangers there in his place, she'd decided to save any but the sketchiest of explanations for another day and had simply gone downstairs to sleep in the spare bedroom with its seldom used and slightly musty mattress. It felt odd to be bivouacked there, bizarre in fact; but human beings are almost infinitely adaptable, and all it took was a decent night's sleep to serve as transition from a situation that seemed totally untenable and completely weird to one that passed for a new if temporary phase of normal. By breakfast next day, Glenda and Meg and Peter were behaving, if not exactly like old friends, at least like thrown-together roommates who were determined to get along and be considerate.

One by one, all of them still a little bleary-eyed with sleep, they'd straggled into the kitchen in slippers and robes and gone about the ordinary business of starting the day. Meg squeezed oranges. Peter sliced bananas onto bowls of cereal. Glenda made toast. Before the women had had their coffee and Peter his carefully dosed out sips of tea there was very little conversation.

But when they'd moved out into the sunshine and were sitting at the small table near the pool, Meg, with a wry flourish, raised her glass of orange juice and said, "So. Well. Here we are."

Tardily but with a sleepy smile, Glenda raised her own glass and they clinked. "Here we are," she agreed.

Here we are? thought Peter. Well, just where the hell was that? Tweaked by his nervousness, he needed to get a few things figured out immediately. "Look," he blurted, "this is really pretty awkward and I don't know what we should do."

"Maybe we should have our breakfast," said his wife.

"I mean," Peter said to Glenda, "your husband's supposedly at our place in New York, but we can't find him. You apparently can't find him either. In the meantime it's not right we're inconveniencing you. But it's high season here and I don't think we could find a hotel room even if we wanted to. So I just don't know what we should do. Maybe we should just leave after breakfast."

Glenda was eating some cereal and for a moment said nothing. Without her high shoes, and with her rather big hair flattened by the pillow, she really wasn't much taller than average. Nor, in the light of morning, did she look like any sort of tough-talking, vase-throwing Mafia moll. Her makeup was gone except for a random smudge of lipstick and her unadorned face was soft and almost girlish. She mostly kept her eyes down and actually seemed a little bashful. Finally, she said simply, "There's no need for you to leave. I like it that you're here."

She said it softly, humbly, as if she was asking a favor rather than stating a fact, and it didn't quite seem to register with Peter.

"At the very least," he went on in a businesslike way, "we should swap rooms until we can figure out another plan. You should have the master. I mean, it's your house, after all."

Glenda put down her spoon and her eyes welled up. She briefly looked around the yard. The skyflower and the allamanda were in bloom. The frangipani tree in the corner had sprouted a single pink blossom on a naked stump of limb. She said, "It doesn't feel like my house right now. Benny isn't here. The cat isn't here. It just doesn't feel like home."

Peter had no idea what to say to that. Meg responded not with a word but a gesture; she put a comforting hand on Glenda's wrist. That light touch was enough to earn Glenda's eternal trust and gratitude, to let her feel she'd found a friend, and all the things she hadn't got around to talking about the night before suddenly came pouring out.

"You know," she said, "the whole ride down the Keys I was imagining how I'd surprise my Benny. I'd sneak into the house, come up the stairs in the dark, stop outside the bedroom door. Probably I'd hear him snoring. I'd tiptoe closer so I could smell him. He smells like bread when he's asleep. I don't know why. He doesn't smell like bread when he's awake. When he's asleep he smells like bread. It never even dawned on me that maybe he wouldn't be here. I never thought that for a second. I hate not knowing where he is."

Meg was patting the back of Glenda's hand. "He'll turn up," she said. "You'll find him."

Glenda's lower lip was trembling. "I was an idiot to leave. I was an idiot to stay away so long. What was I trying to prove? That I don't need him? Except I do."

Meg said, "Come on, think good thoughts. It'll all work out."

Glenda tried to think good thoughts but the effort made her start to sniffle.

After a moment Meg said, "Hey, I have an idea. I haven't been to the beach yet down here. Crazy, right, not to get to the beach? You have a favorite? A local's spot? Maybe after breakfast you could show me. Whaddya say? Feel like chilling out a little?"

Upstairs, in the privacy of the master bedroom, Peter said, "The beach? Our whole life is upside down and you're going to the beach?"

Meg was slipping into a not too revealing two-piece and a bright yellow cotton cover-up. "I thought it would be good for Glenda," she said. "Get her mind off things."

Peter was pacing short laps at the foot of the bed. "Ah, very Zen. Get your mind off things. Home invasions. AWOL husbands. Just rid yourself of negative thoughts and everything will turn out fine."

"You have a better idea?"

"Yeah. For starters, how about we find Benny and find out if there's a fucking cat dropping hairballs all over our apartment?"

Meg was putting sunblock on her nose and cheeks. She looked at Peter in the mirror. "We've tried finding Benny. Benny apparently does not want to be found. What's the point of sitting around obsessing about it?"

"The point..." Peter began, then realized he had nowhere to go with it.

"Look," said Meg, "put yourself in Glenda's place."

"We are in Glenda's place."

"Can't you see how upset she is? How alone? She comes to realize she made a terrible mistake in walking out. She swallows her pride and comes back on this desperate mission to try again. You see how brave that is? She has no idea if he still wants her back. Maybe he's even taken up with someone else by now. But she risks it. Drives down here on this rollercoaster of hope and fear—"

"Very touching," Peter interrupted. "Must-see daytime television. But you're getting all wrapped up in this romantic melodrama and we haven't even told her about the coconut yet. Don't you think she should know about the coconut?"

"There's time for that."

"You sure? When those footsteps were coming up the stairs last night it didn't seem like there was much time left for anything except cremation."

"Right. And we all survived. And nobody got hurt. Except Glenda, who's devastated that her husband isn't here. Come on, Peter, think about it, have some sympathy. You and I, maybe we're not very special people, maybe we're just a sort of average normal couple, but I have you, you have me, we have each other. Glenda has nobody right now. And I think people who have nobody deserve a little extra kindness. Don't you?"

She kissed him on the cheek and headed out.

12.

Benny Bufano, a cup of lukewarm coffee at his side, sat in the Kaplans' living room, just opposite the little alcove where the globe was, doodling in a small notebook he almost always carried with him. He was drawing faces; or rather the same face every time, though from different angles and with different shadings. He was doing this mainly to keep his mind off where he was and why he was there.

To Benny, being in the Kaplans' place was like being stuck in a foreign country he didn't much like. Nothing worked quite the way he was used to. The coffeemaker had given him trouble. It was one of those fancy plunger jobs, and when he plunged it undissolved coffee grounds overflowed like lava and the coffee tasted muddy. There was no television in the living room, just shelves and shelves of books amid the gloomy furniture that was all in shades of brown. The only television was a crummy small one in the bedroom and it wasn't even hooked up to cable. There were paintings on the wall that didn't look like anything but paint.

But of all the things that Benny didn't like about being in the Kaplans' condo, the most galling one by far was that it had never been his idea to be there in the first place. The whole thing had been thought up, as usual, by his father-in-law—the mastermind, the sometime benefactor, the control freak, the tyrant. Frank Fortuna had thought of everything: having Benny turn off his phone so there'd be no government snooping into where he'd been and who he'd spoken with; having him drive, not fly, from Key West to New York so there'd be no record of his having gone there; ditto staying in a home exchange rather than a hotel; and, tidiest of all, finding an apartment just around the corner from that of the person he'd been sent to kill.

In all, it was a well-laid plan, and except for Benny's squeamishness about committing a cold-blooded murder, it really could have been a pretty simple job. Follow Lydia Greenspan home or ambush her as she left her building. Force her into the car, ice her at leisure, and dispose of the body in time-honored fashion somewhere along the New Jersey Turnpike. This would not even require much of a detour or so much as an extra toll as he headed back to Florida. The only problem was that Benny was not at all sure he'd be able to pull the trigger.

So he sat there in the Kaplans' dull and genteel living room and thought about his options. None of them was appetizing. The path of least resistance was to kill Lydia and be done with it. But he was afraid that if he did that he would never again have a night's sleep free of gruesome dreams. If, on the other hand, he balked at icing Lydia, the first thing that would happen is that Mikey would kill his cat, unless the cat had starved to death already. A distressing thought, but okay, it was just a cat. The bigger problem was that Benny would be in deep trouble with Fortuna, a position that generally proved fatal. True, as the big man's son-in-law Benny might reasonably expect some leniency. But was he really family any more? Technically he and Glenda were still married. But she'd left him and she'd shown no sign whatsoever of coming back. Over the past weeks she'd ignored his pleas to talk things over. Chances are she'd told her father she never wanted to see him again. Well, that could be arranged, and a lot more efficiently than by divorce. Then again, if Glenda didn't love him anymore, how much did it really matter what happened to him? Not much. Since she'd left, he hadn't even felt like he'd been living, just going through the motions. Sleepwalking through the days. Faking attention, pretending interest. Missing her pushed everything else off to the side and into the shadows.

Now he closed his little notebook, finished his muddy coffee, and got ready to head down to Grand Central to stalk his prey and eat some more oysters that he didn't want. Going through the motions. Starting the job and vaguely hoping that he wouldn't have to finish it. He had no other plan.

"So here's the crazy part," Glenda was saying. "The crazy part is that until just a few days ago, it was Benny who was trying to get us back together. He kept calling, he wanted to talk. I was so stubborn I wouldn't even listen. As soon as the calls stopped, I was desperate to have him back. Crazy, right? Shit, maybe I *am* crazy."

"You're not crazy," Meg said soothingly. "You're going through a rough patch. It happens."

The two of them, side by side on big pink towels, were hanging out at Fort Zach, Key West's best beach and also its strangest. It was hidden behind some Navy property and situated right next to the harbor entrance, which featured a ship channel that had been dredged extremely close to shore. The result was that at Fort Zach you could often have a stunning panoramic vista of twinkling turquoise sea and in the very next moment a gigantic cruise ship would loom up and you would feel that you were about to be run over, right there on your towel, by a city.

"I've tried to go into therapy," Glenda said. "Couple times, in fact. First was after my Mom died. I was seventeen. No Mom. No sibs. All these mixed up feelings about my father. Poster child for therapy, right? My father said, 'No way. I don't want some quack with a diploma on the wall knowing all about you, all about our family.' I said, 'Pop, they're sworn to secrecy.' He said, 'So was Joe Valachi. Forget about it. You have problems, honey, things on your mind, you talk to me.'"

A pair of jet-skis roared past, kidney-slamming across the wakes of bigger boats. An errant Frisbee bounced and scratched across the sand. Glenda rubbed more sunblock onto her legs and went on.

"That's really kind of funny, right? My father's the issue and he's also the only person I'm allowed to talk to. Where's that going? So I don't think I ever quite grew up. How could I? My father handling everything, protecting me. Then delivering a husband right to the dining room table. Not that Benny was exactly a grownup either. Poor Benny."

"Why poor Benny?" Meg said, and the question had just a bit of an edge to it, since she'd already taken Glenda's side.

"Oh, the usual. Shitty parents. Drunk father, depressed mother. So to get out of the house he falls in with a certain crowd and tries to be accepted by doing what they do and kind of tries to believe that's what it means to be a man. Except he knows it's wrong. Of course he does. I sensed that right away. That's probably why I fell for him instead of one of the bigger, stronger guys. Benny, you see his doubts. He thinks he can hide them but he can't. You see he wants a different life but just doesn't know how to make it happen.

"Like, okay, here's an example," she went on. "Not long before I walked out he tells me he's got an idea for a legitimate business. I say great, I'm thrilled, what is it? He wouldn't tell me, just that it was legit. Fine. So who does he go to to try and make it happen? This local bigshot

Carlos Guzman, who's probably as crooked as my father. That made me furious. But it was also sad. Like, these are the only kinds of people he knows how to talk to?"

She broke off. In her frustration she'd been digging holes in the sand with her feet. She took a moment to fill them in and smooth them over and then began again. "He means well. I know he does. That's the part that kills me. I just wish we didn't fight so much."

Meg sat up and squinted out to sea. A spray of small fish broke the surface as they fled from something that was trying to eat them. A distant buoy rocked hypnotically in the current. "Wha'd you fight about?" she asked.

"Anything," said Glenda. "Nothing. We just fought. It was stupid. Childish. And we both knew it. That's the second time I pushed for therapy. Marriage counseling. I say to Benny, 'Let's talk to someone, let's try at least to figure out why we can't stop arguing.' And Benny's answer is just like my father's. 'No one needs to know our business.' But here's the thing. He wanted the counseling as much as I did. Maybe even more. I could see it in his eyes. He just couldn't let himself do it...But jeez, I'm sorry, I'm talking way too much. I really don't have girlfriends, I don't get to talk like this. How about you? You have girlfriends that you talk to?"

Meg took a moment to think it over. Sure, she had buddies from the yoga studio and her assorted jobs, women with whom she shared the occasional lunch and lots of pleasant chit-chat. But when it came to really talking, really airing things out, the person she spoke with was her husband.

"What a concept!" Glenda said, when her new friend had explained this. "Conversation. Maybe Benny and I can try that sometime." She gave one of her wry and wistful shrugs, then hugged her knees and looked out to sea. "I mean, a girl can dream, can't she?"

13.

Special Agent Andy Sheehan, ramrod straight and confident as always, stood without a topcoat in front of the gleaming Park Avenue tower in which the too-successful trader Marc Orlovsky had his offices. It was lunchtime and droves of people were streaming through revolving doors, hailing taxis, slipping into limousines or spotless SUVs. Most wandered off in twos and threes, little knots of friends or colleagues chatting, laughing. When Orlovsky appeared he was alone.

He was a dark-haired man of average size but there was something subliminally unpleasant in his looks. This was mainly to do with his posture. His head hung slightly too far forward, buzzard-like, and though he wasn't fat his sloping shoulders made him look dumpy in his three thousand dollar custom suit. His chin was too thick and it hung pinkly over the edge of his snug collar. Sheehan watched him from fifty yards away as he paused briefly on the sidewalk, glanced casually around him, then started strolling south. He weaved through the crowds and dodged bike messengers at the cross streets, and the agent had no trouble tailing him to the foot of Park Avenue, through the teeming lobbies of the Helmsley and the Met Life buildings, and down the escalator to the vast and soaring atrium of Grand Central.

Once inside the terminal, Orlovsky seemed to grow more cautious, more tentative. He meandered past the ticket windows, checked his watch, glanced up now and then at the splendid vaulted ceiling with its painted constellations, perused the timetables, checked his watch again. By this shuffling, serpentine sort of progress he made his way over to the famous four-faced clock just as a very ordinary-looking woman in a simple cloth coat was reaching it by way of a staircase from the lower level. They met as if by chance and stood together for not more than twenty seconds. They exchanged a few brief words, then the woman handed Orlovsky a tiny piece of paper, a scrap no bigger than a stamp. The trader appeared to read it very quickly, then brought his hand to his mouth and walked away.

Sheehan saw it all, but he'd been so intent on witnessing the transaction that he failed to notice that someone else was observing it as well. Benny Bufano, queasy from the combination of stress and oysters and racing up the stairs to get a step ahead of the woman in the cloth coat, had been watching from the mezzanine.

Each reasonably satisfied with the progress of the day's surveillance, each oblivious to the other's presence, the FBI man and the hit man discreetly turned to follow their respective targets and walked off in opposite directions.

At JB's Grouper Wagon, Peter, lunching alone, had claimed a high stool at the counter that flanked the sidewalk and was waiting for his sandwich. Like most people when they eat alone, he was slightly uncomfortable, had some trouble deciding what to do with his hands. He fiddled with the napkin dispenser, looked around for something to read, a newspaper, a flyer, anything. There was nothing so he just watched the parade of people going by. A few were dressed more or less like Hollywood's idea of pirates. One had a cockatoo crapping down his shoulder. The afternoon had crossed over from warm to hot and the countertop smelled like dried ketchup. Trying to look like he was relaxed and having fun, Peter secretly wondered why he didn't enjoy vacations more. He knew he was supposed to look forward to them but then he seldom enjoyed them. It was a conundrum.

Preoccupied with this riddle, he was surprised when he heard a soft, deep voice just behind him and to his right. "This seat taken?"

He wheeled and saw the old man with the little dog who'd been at JB's the day before. "Oh, hi. Bert, right?"

"Right," the old man said, offering a papery hand and settling with more caution than he wanted to show onto the high stool. "And you're the individual who was extremely curious about a certain person who we mutually agreed we wouldn't talk too much about. Where's your lovely wife today?"

"The beach."

"Nice day for it. What about you? You also allergic to a little sunshine?"

"Actually," said Peter, "she went with a friend."

"You got friends down here? That's nice."

Peter's sandwich arrived. Aromas of fried fish and onions curled up from the plate. He pushed it aside and dropped his voice to a confidential murmur. "Actually, she went with Glenda Bufano."

At that, Bert cradled his chihuahua a little more snugly against his middle. His face took on a look that was not exactly suspicious but bore a suggestion of who-is-kidding-who-here. "Wait a second," he said. "So you do know the Bufanos?"

"We know Glenda," Peter said, "as of about one o'clock this morning." He told Bert about the odd circumstances of her unexpected arrival at her own house. Then he finally picked up his sandwich.

"So lemme make sure I have this right," the old man said. "They're on the outs, but Glenda comes to Key West on the erroneous though understandable assumption that she will find him here. Except she doesn't."

"Right," said Peter.

Bert's lunch arrived. He fed the dog a couple of black beans before he had anything himself. "Two lousy beans, dog's gonna fart all afternoon," he said, "but that's life." As an aside to the dog, he said, "You're a big little farter, ain't ya?" Then, turning his attention back to the subject of Benny, he went on, "So Glenda can't reach him, you can't reach him, he don't call anybody back."

"That's about it."

"Sounds like he's gone whaddyacallit...wha' do people say these days? Off the griddle."

"Off the grid," said Peter.

"Griddle, grid, he ain't in touch with nobody. This would tend to suggest or let's say indicate that he is on let's say an errand."

"What kind of errand?"

This was a gauche question and Bert's only answer was to bite into his sandwich.

"Like, a dangerous errand?" Peter pressed.

With surprising daintiness Bert wiped his big lips on a napkin. "How should I know?" He fed the dog a morsel of grouper, which the dog captured on a pink tongue about half the length of its body. "But talk about dangerous—the most dangerous job in America, know what it is? Garbageman. More garbagemen get hurt on the job than firemen and cops put together. Maybe killed too. Read that somewhere, can't remember where. Don't know if garbage falls on them, they fall off the truck when it goes around a corner...Don't know."

"Very interesting," said Peter. "But about Benny—"

Bert stopped him with a raised hand and a forbearing look such as a teacher might direct toward a willing but ungifted student. "It appears like you didn't notice that I was trying to gently move the conversation away from a subject that I find personally inappropriate and not suited to the occasion of lunchtime in a public place with an individual I hardly know."

Peter, chastened, went back to his sandwich.

After a moment, Bert, giving some ground, went on. "Look, I have no idea what Benny's up to, I really don't. But it's none of your business and, trust me, you don't want it to become your business. So my entirely friendly and amicable advice is don't ask too many questions and don't get involved."

Peter certainly saw the wisdom in the old man's counsel. Except it seemed a little too late to follow it. "But we are sort of involved," he said. "We're living in his house. We're sort of babysitting his wife."

Bert gave his head a sympathetic shake. "She's a good kid, Glenda. Messed up, but who could blame her? Nice that you've kind of adopted her."

Adopted her? The very notion gave Peter a sharp stab of worry deep in his gut, a little south of where the grouper sandwich was now heavily sitting. "Wait a second. Let's not make it sound like suddenly it's one big happy family. She and my wife went to the beach, that's all."

"Nice that you're standing by her in her hour of need."

"Hour of need? You said ten seconds ago we shouldn't get

involved!" protested Peter.

"Right. But that was before you admitted you already was. That changes everything. You're already involved, you gotta do the right thing."

"I do? Who says I do?"

"Nobody says it. Everybody knows it. You're in a situation, you handle it right. Lemme know if I can help. Tell Glenda she can call me anytime. She knows how to reach me."

14.

Behind the closed door of his tiny office with its crappy lighting and crummy desk, Andy Sheehan was showing Lou Duncan the photographs he'd taken earlier that day with a camera in his tie-tack. Mockingly, he said, "You see? You *see?* There's your thoroughly modern white collar criminal, your cyber genius, your ultra-savvy market manipulator. I mean, can you believe this shit? She's handing him a piece of *paper.*"

Duncan sidled around the desk to get a better angle on the screen of Sheehan's beat up and archaic laptop. "Yup," he said, "it sure looks like she's handing him something."

"Wait, it gets better," Sheehan said, clicking to another image. "Shit, how do you get this thing to zoom?"

Duncan took over the keyboard and showed Sheehan for the twentieth time how the zoom feature worked.

"Okay, stop," the tall agent said. "There it is. There it is."

He pointed at the now blurred close-up of Marc Orlovsky's face. The grotesquely swollen pixels made it appear that the stock trader's skin was decomposing and sloughing off, but the action of the image was plain enough.

"He's eating the evidence!" Sheehan said with a kind of glee. "He's chewing, for Christ's sake!" Then he pointed vaguely toward the office of the younger agent whom he had for some reason decided was his personal nemesis. "Our Boy Wonder is chasing the guy with super-computers or video games or whatever the hell he's doing, and meantime the guy is getting information and eating it like it's 1937."

Duncan clicked back to a previous image. "Who's the woman?"

"No idea," said Sheehan. "Yet."

"Player? Go-between? Decoy?"

"Decoy, I don't think so," Sheehan said. "Not unless Orlovsky has a thing for eating paper. Player or messenger. Ask me again in a day or two. I'll know more about her than she knows about herself."

Back from the beach, Meg and Glenda had showered, rubbed themselves with various après-sun emollients, and reconvened at the shady table by the pool for a refreshing glass of pinot grigio. But as they were toasting their new friendship Meg decided that it was no longer fair or practical to keep from Glenda the disturbing facts about the broken window. Putting down her wineglass, she said, "Excuse me a sec. I need to show you something."

In a moment she came back with the scarred and battered coconut. Its greenish husk had been slowly drying out and seemed a bit more bruised and wrinkled than it had the day before. Presenting it to Glenda like a court exhibit, she said, "Someone threw this into the house a couple nights ago."

Glenda slowly reached a hand toward the projectile but didn't seem to want to touch it. In a heartbeat the rosy glow of sunburn began receding from her skin and left her looking blanched.

"There's some writing on it," Meg went on, and she twirled the coconut so Glenda could see the facet where the message was. As she tried to make out the words and ferret out the meaning amid the smudges and the non-existent grammar, her jaw got tenser and her hands curled gradually into fists. After a pause she said three words. "My fucking father."

She stormed off to the guest bedroom and called him up.

In the Naples mansion, the call came through on the only phone Frank Fortuna actually answered, the one with the special ring reserved for his daughter and for no one else. He picked it up at once. "Glenda," he said, "where are you? Are you okay?"

"Where's Benny?" she countered.

"The hell with Benny. Tell me where you are."

"Where's Benny," she said again.

"Glenda, stop it! Tell me why you just took off like that. I've been worried sick."

"I doubt it," Glenda said, though it happened to be true. After a moment she relented. "Okay. Okay. I'm in Key West and I came here because I didn't want to live one more day without my husband. You got that? You understand?"

Fortuna couldn't find an answer for a moment and his daughter raged on.

"Weird stuff is going on down here. Benny can't be reached. I got strangers in my house. I got people breaking windows. Just what the hell is going on?"

Stalling for time, trying to organize his thoughts and come up with a passable evasion, Fortuna said, "I thought you were through with Benny. I thought it was over."

"It isn't over. It'll never be over. I love him. And if anything happens to him—"

"Now, honey—" her father broke in quickly. He didn't want to hear what she might say next, and Glenda herself didn't know what the words might be, only that if she didn't slow down a bit they might be something reckless and perhaps irreparable.

She took a quick short breath and said, "You're making him do something bad, aren't you? I know you are. That's what everything points to. You promised me you wouldn't."

"I never promised that," said Fortuna. He fancied himself a man who kept his word, and whenever it was pointed out to him that he had broken a promise his impulse was to revise history as necessary, often by just a slight re-phrasing. "What I promised was that I would look out for him. And I have. For years."

"So what about now?"

Fortuna went silent for a moment. He'd lived and prospered by shrewdly reading people and accurately if cynically appraising situations, and it galled him to realize he'd gotten it so wrong as to where things stood between his own daughter and his son-in-law. Trying to shift some of the blame, he said, "You told me you didn't want to be with him anymore. You said all kinds of awful things about him."

"I'm his wife," said Glenda. "I'm entitled to."

There was a standoff, nothing passing between father and daughter except an occasional soft crackle of static. As the seconds ticked by, Glenda felt herself not softening exactly, but slipping backwards toward a childish pouting helplessness that she absolutely hated. With her father she either hissed or purred, and she'd used up all her hissing for the moment. "Daddy," she said, "please don't let anything happen to Benny. Whatever's going on, please, you have to fix it. You have to make it right."

With a sigh that was meant to sound both magnanimous and wise, Fortuna said, "I'll try my best."

But even as he said it he knew he wouldn't try at all. Things had gone too far to change them now. There was crew morale and respect to be considered. The troublesome Lydia Greenspan had to be taken off the street, and soon. Benny had to finish what he'd started, or rather, what Fortuna had started for him. Unless he botched the job it shouldn't be that big a deal, it would all blow over, and besides, there really was no other way.

"Thank you, Daddy," Glenda purred. "I knew you'd understand."

15.

Benny Bufano was not a morning drinker, but next day, hoping to appease his shattered nerves and to uncover some courage or at least some cruelty deep within himself, he had a big belt of the Kaplans' Irish whiskey with his muddy coffee. He felt no better and no different after the drink. He realized that in sucking whiskey on the morning of a job he was just going through the motions, doing what he believed a person in his situation ought to do. But it was automatic and it was false. It wasn't him.

This sense of faking it, of disconnection, unwholesome as it was, carried certain advantages as well. The main one was an extreme dispassionate clarity. Benny might barely have recognized himself, but he grasped in minute detail what needed to be done. At ten-fifteen he began to dress; by twenty-five after his shoulder holster was in place, snugly bearing the cold weight of the never-registered, never-fired 9 mm that Frank Fortuna had provided for the job. At ten-thirty he gathered up his few belongings and made a cursory inspection of the Kaplans' apartment. A considerate guest in spite of everything, he removed a chest hair from the bathroom sink and rubbed away a moisture ring on the kitchen counter before turning his back on the place and leaving without a shred of fondness.

Outside on West End Avenue it was freezing cold under a white sky smudged here and there with pasty yellow. Benny's breath steamed but he hardly noticed. He retrieved his car from its overpriced garage up on Amsterdam and set out on the most delicately-timed aspect of the entire operation: Gaming the alternate-side parking rules. Falling into a line of crawling vehicles as they trailed a street-sweeper whose huge brushes were scratching at the curbs of 93rd Street, he scored a space right in front of Lydia Greenspan's building, just where, if her patterns held, she'd be stepping out of a taxi within a couple hours.

Benny switched his radio on, took out his little notebook, and sketched Glenda's face with a dozen different expressions while he waited.

On Poorhouse Lane it was another sunny and salt-scented morning but there was a mini-crisis going on. Amidst all the tumult and the upsets no one had got around to buying groceries and the household had run out of milk. No milk for coffee, no milk for tea, no milk for cereal. And no one felt like running to the store. So Peter volunteered to see if the neighbor, Mel, could spare some milk.

He slipped through the foliage in the side yard and found the toothless old man rocking slowly on his porch. Before Peter had even reached the creaky steps, Mel said, "I see you got a nice car by your house now."

Peter said, "Yeah. Glenda came home the other night."

"Just Glenda? No Benny?"

"Just Glenda."

The old man sucked his gums and winked. "So you got, like, a ménage going on over there?"

"No, nothing like that."

"Me, I've done some threesomes back in the day. Baja. The Azores, twice. Rio. Rio was a sister act. Said they were sisters, at least. Didn't look that much alike. Marketing gimmick probably. One of 'em—"

"I'm sure it was fun," Peter broke in, "but I was wondering if you could spare a little milk."

"Yeah, it was fun. But overrated, y'ask me. Y'ask me, guys do it more for bragging rights than pussy."

"So why'd you do it four times?" Peter could not help asking.

"Guess I liked it. Still, you're paying double and then it's like you're at a big buffet. Lots to choose from, but it's still one meal. Am I right?"

"Um, right," said Peter. "But about the milk..."

"Oh sure, sure, help yourself," said Mel, and he gestured toward the ravaged screen door with the silhouette of the flamingo on it. "Kitchen's straight back. Milk, I use the box kind. Lasts forever. Grab one from the cabinet right next to the fridge."

Peter stepped into the house and was immediately enveloped in the funk of mildew and the toasted sawdust smell left behind by gnawing termites. Dim light straggled in through narrow, dirty windows. There were dented pans piled in the kitchen sink and the knob on the cabinet where the milk was was gritty to the touch. It was not until Peter had grabbed the milk and was heading out again that he saw the guns hanging on the wall near the front door.

There were three of them. They had dings and dents and rust spots here and there. They didn't match. Guns worried Peter. He knew nothing about them and he didn't want to know. He glanced at them for just a moment then hurried back into the daylight.

On the porch again, Mel said, "You like my souvenirs?"

"Hm?"

"The semi-automatics. Everybody stops to look at them. How can you not?"

Peter had nothing to say to that.

"A lot of these hellholes," his host went on, "you go ashore, there really isn't much to do. Get drunk, wet your wood if you're lucky, buy some souvenirs."

"Some people buy t-shirts," Peter observed. "Refrigerator magnets. Little flags."

"Busted weapons, they're always getting left behind. Most of 'em, you can buy 'em for a song. Something's jammed, a piece or two is missing, whatever. That vintage M-14 is from Saigon when it was still Saigon. The AK-47 I picked up in Algiers along with a nasty case of crabs. The Uzi came from Mogadishu. My pension ever runs out, I'll sell 'em on eBay. Someone could probably fix 'em up just fine."

"Good," said Peter. "Good idea. Well, I better bring the milk home now."

"Yeah, back to your harem."

"No, just back to my cereal."

He headed down the creaking steps and his host called out to his retreating back. "Hey, y'ever need some help with the ladies over there, don't forget old Mel."

At Grand Central Terminal, Andy Sheehan watched from a discreet distance through a blurring curtain of hurrying people as Marc Orlovsky had another brief rendezvous with the mysterious woman in the simple cloth coat. As before, the agent clearly saw the exchange of information and the archaic spectacle of the stock trader choking down a morsel of paper. But this time, when the momentary tete-a-tete was over, it was the woman that he followed.

She turned without hesitation toward the west side of the building, her mid-heels clicking softly on the well-scuffed floor. At the Vanderbilt Avenue exit she pushed against a glass and metal door—pushed hard, the way New Yorkers, accustomed to difficulty, to resistance, pushed— and emerged onto the sidewalk. She paused very briefly for a single deep gulp of bracing winter air then headed for the lead taxi in a standing rank.

Sheehan waited until the target car was pulling away from the curb then slid into the one behind it. Softly but with urgency, he said, "Follow that taxi. Not too close."

His driver, who seemed to be recently arrived from somewhere on the Indian subcontinent, was clearly delighted with the request. Swiveling backward and smiling broadly at his fare, he said, "Wow, you mean *tail him*, like on TV or in the movies?"

Sheehan pointed forward toward the street, where the other taxi was already half a block ahead. "Yeah, like in the movies. Don't lose him."

The driver, beaming, turned back toward the steering wheel and gripped it tightly. *"Follow that car!"* he mused aloud. *"Step on it, Mac!* This is so amazing, so wonderful. I'm just a simple man from a small village. Who could have even dreamed that such a wonderful thing could happen to me here?" He put the car in gear and with a gusto that pinned Sheehan against his seat-back, he shot out from the curb and into midtown traffic.

16.

"Due respect," said Bert, "I've never liked your father."

He and Glenda were sitting out by the pool, Meg and Peter having discreetly gone out for a bike ride. An afternoon breeze put tiny ripples in the water and the skimmer made a soft sucking sound as the wavelets ebbed and flowed.

"'Course," the old man went on, stroking the chihuahua in his lap, "he never liked me neither. Nah, lemme rephrase that. There came a particular moment in time when he immediately stopped liking me or at least pretending that he liked me and started very obviously hating my guts."

"Why?" asked Glenda. "What happened?"

"Happened?" said Bert. "Nothing happened. It was just something I said to him. I made the basic, fundamental error of telling him the truth. I told him he was a fucking hypocrite. Pardon my French."

"You said that to my father?" She couldn't quite keep a note of awe and maybe vindication out of her voice. She'd never heard anyone except herself say anything but fawning, cautious words to Frank Fortuna. Then again, if anyone would have had the gall to tell him off, Bert d'Ambrosia—known to everyone inside as Bert the Shirt, for his splendid if eccentric wardrobe—would have been the guy. Bert did things no one else would even try, up to and including retiring from the Mob. He'd got out on a technicality: He'd dropped dead years before on the courthouse steps and flat-lined for around ten seconds, thereby fulfilling his oath to be loyal till he died. After that he was once again his own man, free.

"Yeah, I said that to him," Bert answered. "Look, there's nothing wrong with trying to improve yourself. Hey, we all do that. Me, I do crosswords, sometimes I look up big words in the dictionary. Contraindicated. Pusillanimous. That's different than forgetting who you are, pretending like you never were that guy. What, you play golf, you're not a goombah anymore? Where'd you come from, fucking Scarsdale, fucking Greenwich? That's bullshit. Your father didn't like having that pointed out...But okay, ancient history. What's going on with you? You and Benny, I hear you're on the outs."

"We are. We were. But I want to patch it up. We're meant for each other, Bert, it can't be any other way. Except I can't find him. That's why I called you. Maybe you can help."

Bert petted his dog and gallantly said he would if he could. The dog for some reason picked that moment to stand up in the old man's lap and pirouette, its tiny feet dancing all around his crotch.

Glenda reached behind her and produced the much-examined coconut that had come smashing into the living room. Handing it over, she said, "I wonder what you make of this."

Lydia Greenspan was paying her cab fare. Absorbed in the routine business of counting her change and calculating a tip, she took no notice of the short but thickly built man who just then was sliding out of the driver's seat of his car and positioning himself between her taxi and the entrance to her building. Oblivious to any danger, she opened the cab door and swung her legs out in that prim and careful way that women do. She closed the door and the taxi pulled away. Benny was on her before she reached the curb.

He may not have been a killer in his heart of hearts but he was very strong and he had skills. In one quick and fluid motion he wrenched Lydia's wrist behind her back and with the other hand he pressed the muzzle of his pistol hard against her kidney. Prodding with the gun, pushing with his knees against the backs of his quarry's trembling legs, he said in a ferocious whisper, "Into the car, Lydia. One sound, one move, you're dead. Open the door and get in."

Oddly numb, numb not as from novocaine but from a paralyzing electric shock, she tried to do as she was told but her body wouldn't move. Benny pushed and folded her into the front seat. The inside handle had been removed from the passenger door and there was a handcuff latched onto the armrest. Benny slapped the other cuff on Lydia's wrist, bustled around to the driver's side, and screeched away. The abduction took ten seconds.

It took fifteen for Andy Sheehan's taxi to make the turn across

Broadway onto 93rd Street, and by the time it reached the scene the agent could not be remotely sure what he was witnessing. The cab he'd been following had vanished. A car with a Florida license plate was careening onto West End Avenue, heading south. There seemed to be a woman in the front seat of the car, though at the distance of three quarters of a block he could not be sure if it was the same woman he'd been tailing. If it wasn't, where had his target gotten to so quickly? And if it was, why had she taken a taxi all the way uptown only to head down again at once?

Sheehan squandered a few precious seconds puzzling it out, then by instinct more than thought he screamed at his driver to follow the Florida car. The driver whooped and grinned and shouted things in Urdu as he hurtled down the street. But the chase, hindered at nearly every corner by West Siders shuffling along with canes and walkers and strollers and cellos, proved futile. Sheehan gave it up at 72nd Street with nothing gained except a tag number, and Benny and his prisoner continued on toward the Lincoln Tunnel and the dumping ground that was New Jersey.

Bert said sagely, "I make of it that it's a coconut."

"Someone threw it through a window the other night," Glenda told him.

The old man sadly shook his head. "Our friends, why are they so primitive in their chosen way of sending messages? Other people, they want to send a message, they write an email, they post a twit on Tweeter. Our guys, it's always the broken window, the dead fish, the horse's head. What's with that already?"

"There's writing," Glenda said, and she twirled the coconut so Bert could see the scrawls.

He studied them carefully, even running his papery fingertips over the nicks and dents.

"*She dies you die,*" Glenda recited. "Who's *she?*"

"Of that I have no idea."

"And these little markings here and there. It's exasperating. She dies *and* you die? *If* she dies you die? What the hell does it mean?"

Bert the Shirt grew somber, leaned back in his chair, and stroked his dog like he was rubbing his own chin to help him concentrate. Finally he said, "I'm sorry, Glenda, but I don't think it means either of those things. I know your father pretty well. He likes to give people, whaddyacallit, ultimatums. Like two stinking choices, pick one."

"So..."

"So I think it means she dies *or* you die."

Glenda seemed to fend off understanding for a moment, then she swallowed back a nasty taste that had risen in her throat. At last she said, "So you're saying my Benny comes back a murderer or he doesn't come back at all?"

Bert stayed quiet and the question hovered in the warm blue air above the pool.

17.

In Elizabeth, New Jersey, not far from exit 13 on the Turnpike, there is an area called Bayway that borders a narrow and reeking inlet known as the Arthur Kill and is a very convincing facsimile of Hell. Sickly flames burn in the cracking towers of oil refineries, giving the clouds an orange cast even in the daytime. Rusty tankers and squat, graceless freighters sit jammed together in fetid water that has a morbid rainbow sheen; cranes arrayed at jarring, random angles poke obscenely at the sky. On the fenced and sunken parcels of land not taken up by abandoned factories, junkyards sprout, their metal mountains of detritus growing ever higher, steeper, until their tops collapse and they rain down debris like cold volcanoes.

It was into one of these sprawling and chaotic junkyards that Benny Bufano drove the car in which Lydia Greenspan was captive. Near the gate, sitting on a metal chair and smoking a stub of a cigar, a single employee gave him just the slightest nod as he lumbered past into the bowels of the enormous yard. He rattled over potholes and through viscous puddles the color of anti-freeze, past a precinct of eviscerated washing machines and dryers, and stopped at last near a tower of compacted cars—sedans and station wagons squashed down like panini and tenuously stacked like dirty plates on a waiter's tray. He switched off his ignition, expecting quiet. Instead, the car filled up with the roar and whine of unseen bulldozers and the infernal beep-tones of backing trucks and the screams of scavenging gulls.

For a moment neither the hit man nor his prisoner said a word. Then Benny said softly, "I'm sorry, Lydia. I'm really sorry. This whole thing kind of sucks."

She half-turned in her seat, the handcuffs rattling slightly, and looked toward her captor but not directly at him. Mostly she was gazing without focus at an incongruous plastic figurine of a hula girl in a fake grass skirt that was mounted on the dashboard, and beyond it through the windshield. "I'm from Jersey," she said. "Did you know that? Crappy little town called East Brunswick, maybe fifteen miles from here. Spent my whole life trying to get away. Now I'm back. Ironic, no?"

Benny had not been able to bring himself to look at Lydia on the whole ride from Manhattan, but now he did. She was actually sort of pretty. She had soft brown eyes, tender but not frightened eyes. Her jawline was firm, her neck sturdy but graceful, and her lips were pale but full. Not knowing that he was about to speak aloud, Benny said, "Why'd you do it, Lydia?"

"Do what?"

"Get involved in this. With frauds and mobsters. Why? For the money?"

She put the tip of her tongue at the corner of her mouth and thought it over for a moment. Then she said, "No. Not really. I mean, I had a job. Dullest job in the world. Librarian at a law firm. Lawyers would tell me to look up cases. I'd find the case in a big leather book, stick a bookmark in it, hand it to the lawyer. That was it, that was my job. Paid the rent. But this...this I did for excitement. For fun."

Benny gestured through the windshield at the crushed cars and the garbage. "Fun?"

"Yeah," said Lydia. "For a while. For a while it was the most fun thing in my life. Understand, I'd always been a really good girl. Too good. Didn't shoplift. Never bounced a check. I woke up one morning, thirty-seven, single, boring job, drab apartment, and thought *Why?* Why have I been so fucking good? Because I'm a wonderful person? No. Because I never imagined being any other way. I never *let* myself imagine. From that day on, I started to. It was like a whole new way to be. Breaking rules. Stealing lipsticks. Flirting with danger. It was exciting. One thing led to another and here we are."

"This is a long way from stealing lipsticks," Benny said.

Lydia shrugged, or half-shrugged with the arm that wasn't bound.

Benny drummed softly on the steering wheel. After a moment he said, "So if it wasn't about the money, why'd you ask for more?"

"Hey, I'm not stupid. They were making millions with that information. I just asked for a raise."

"That was a mistake," said Benny. He said it not in a tone of blame but of collegial sympathy.

She looked out at the disembodied fenders and the ruptured engine blocks leaking oil and gave a mirthless little laugh. "Yeah, I see that now."

"People like this," Benny said, "asking for a raise, it's a no-win situation. If you get it, the boss is pissed, he starts thinking about ways to do without you. If you don't get it, then he thinks *you're* pissed and he starts worrying about your loyalty. Starts worrying you might turn. That's why we're here, Lydia. You made him worry."

"Understandable," she said. "I get it." Then, with an almost clinical coolness, she added, "Maybe I got it all along. Maybe I was pushing my luck, asking for trouble. Death wish. Game of chicken. That's possible."

Benny kept drumming very lightly on the steering wheel, the rhythm never changing. "So would you have?" he asked. "Would you have turned?"

"I wasn't planning on it, no. Down the road, who knows what I would've done? This being bad, it's new to me, it's not like I have it all thought out...But how about you? The things you do, the tough guy stuff. It just comes naturally?"

Benny looked down at his thick strong hands and said very softly, "No. Not really."

After that neither of them said anything for what seemed a long while. Outside, gulls cackled and machinery clattered and sulfurous smoke drifted up to mingle with the clouds, but inside the car the awkward silence stretched on. Finally, Lydia said, "I'm getting cold and there's a really nasty smell around here. Maybe we should sort of move this thing along."

Benny said nothing and he didn't move a muscle. Lydia swiveled as far as she could and looked more full on at him than she had before. "Hey," she said, "you're crying."

The hit man didn't answer, just shook his head so hard that the tears flew sideways from the corners of his eyes.

Lydia said, "Come on, pull yourself together. I'm the one who should be crying. Wait, I think I have a Kleenex in my purse."

She managed the clasp with one hand and gave him the Kleenex. He dabbed at his eyes and then he blew his nose and thanked her.

She said, "You're welcome. No offense, but I think maybe you're in the wrong line of work."

He nodded but kept on silently weeping.

"Cheer up," she said. "It's nothing personal. I understand that. This had to happen. It's the way things were meant to play. For both of us. Come on, let's get it over with."

She managed something almost like a smile and gestured with her lifted chin toward the driver's side door. Benny struggled for a deep breath that stuttered and wheezed against the pressure of his quiet sobbing. Then, finally, he slipped out of the car and moved on unsteady legs to Lydia's side. He opened her door, unlocked the handcuffs, and walked her through the stink and the clamor to a place on the far side of a mountain of cars where no one would see the execution.

Moments passed. Gulls screamed. Machinery clanked. When two close-together gunshots finally rang out, their pop and whine added only a paltry and fleeting extra noise to the ceaseless and infernal din.

18.

On their rented bicycles, Peter and Meg had meandered among the flaking, whitewashed tombs and mold-darkened, leaning headstones of the above-ground cemetery; through Bayview Park with its mix of daytime drunks and aging tennis players patched-up with knee-braces and adhesive tape; then across White Street, a funky boulevard that smelled like Cuban coffee and drying laundry, toward the ocean. Against a soft breeze that held a tang of iodine, they pedaled up along the promenade, finally pausing to sit down a while on the knee-high seawall out beyond the airport. Pelicans cruised past them, seeming to mimic incoming planes. Small rays scudded along, sucking up tiny crabs from the muddy bottom and blowing out puffs of silt through their gills. Terns dove, sudden sprays of translucent fish arced above the surface, and then, just opposite from where they sat, a large car with purple-tinted windows abruptly pulled up at the curb.

The passenger door opened; a blast of Latin music and a gust of pine-scented air-conditioning escaped. A big man in fighter-pilot shades stepped out. He wore what appeared to be diamond earrings and his hair was of the length and thickness found in the grass of putting greens, though it was jet black and seemed to have been oiled. He wore tight gray pants and a shiny shirt whose buttons stretched across his chest. He walked up quite close to Meg and Peter and said, "Nice day."

The man's thighs were at the level of their faces and his bulk was nearer than was comfortable. Meg and Peter said nothing.

"Not too humid," the man went on. "Some nice clouds here and there."

He gazed and pointed briefly at the sky then grabbed Peter by the shoulders and pushed him into the ocean.

Peter didn't fall off the seawall all at once. Recoiling from the shove, he strained to grip the concrete with the backs of his legs while whirly-gigging with his arms for balance. He lost altitude a little at a time and ended up slithering more than falling into six inches of softly lapping water. The water was bathtub warm from reflected heat and a little slimy with weeds and algae. Peter sloshed around in it for just a moment as he tried to rise on legs that had turned to jelly from fear and outrage. Then, standing ankle-deep in the ocean and resting his wet forearms on the seawall, he said in a pinched and rasping voice, "What the hell'd you do that for?"

"You're friends with Benny Bufano. I saw you leave his place."

Meg had sidled protectively, defiantly, between the big man and her dripping husband. "We're not friends," she said. "We're just staying at his house."

This didn't wash with the big man, who apparently was unfamiliar with the home-exchanging concept. "Tell him it's very rude to stand someone up for a business meeting."

"Look," said Peter, "we can't tell him anything. We're not in touch with him. We don't know anything about a business meeting. Why does everybody keep giving us messages for Benny?"

The big man had no interest in the broader question and kept on with his own line of thought. "Carlos Guzman is a busy man," he said. "Wasting his time is just not a good idea."

The name sounded vaguely familiar to Meg, though at first she couldn't place it. Then, after a moment she said, "Guzman as in Guzman Glass? Carlos as in Casa Carlos?"

"And many other businesses as well," the big man said with a sort of dog-like pride. "For a little *cabron* like Benny to blow off a meeting with Carlos, not even to call, that was very, very rude."

Meg didn't argue the point but she still felt she held the higher moral ground. She put her hands on her hips and pointed toward her husband standing in the water. "And pushing someone in the ocean, that's polite?"

At that the big man smiled, showing a gold tooth in among the others. "Lady," he said, "you I like. You got some *fuego*. So listen, you just tell your friend Benny he needs to apologize about the meeting. That's all. A nice apology, an explanation, Carlos will listen."

With that, he turned and walked back to the car with the purple-tinted windows. Peter waited until the vehicle had driven off before clambering back over the seawall on his belly.

"Glenda Bufano. Glenda Bufano. That name mean anything to you?" asked Andy Sheehan.

He'd run the Florida license plate and now was standing in Lou Duncan's office, which was just as cramped and crummy as his own, but made less dreary by assorted photos of Duncan's wife and kids. Sheehan, long divorced and childless, kept nothing personal on his desk and shelves.

"Um, offhand, no," said Duncan. He said it rather distractedly because he was doing some work of his own at the time. Sheehan seemed not to notice this.

"Eighteen Poorhouse Lane," he went on, "Key West, Florida."

Duncan said nothing and kept trying to get some work done.

"Just wish I could be sure it was the same woman in that car," Sheehan mused. "I think it must have been. But why?"

He started pacing back and forth in front of Duncan's desk. The motion created a slight breeze that rustled the other agent's papers.

"It makes no sense," he went on, "unless…Unless she was in that car against her will."

At that Lou Duncan finally looked up. "Against her will, as in kidnapped?"

"Maybe."

"You saw a woman being kidnapped and you didn't send out an APB?"

"I didn't see it. I'm saying maybe. Besides, I send out an APB, what does it accomplish?"

"What it accomplishes," said Duncan, "is that maybe it saves this woman's life."

That didn't seem to count for much in Sheehan's reckoning. In his certain and unwavering view, the woman was a criminal, end of story, she deserved what she got. Then again, alive she might prove very useful as an informant. But only if properly managed. "Right," he said, "and some rookie patrolman makes the bust and handles it badly and blows the thing wide open and there goes our case against Orlovsky."

"Our case?" Duncan said. "Your case. Except it isn't, remember?"

Sheehan had started pacing again. "Bufano, Bufano. Wasn't there some low-level guy named that? Years ago. Never had anything on him, just knew he was associated. Lenny? Bobby? Something like that."

Trying to get back to his own work, Duncan said, "Ask your young friend the computer whiz. He's got the best database."

"I wouldn't ask him for a toothpick," Sheehan snarled. He paced a few more laps, then said, "But say it was a kidnapping. Why is someone from Florida suddenly in the middle of a scam that's totally New York?"

Duncan's only answer was to square up some papers. Sheehan didn't take the hint.

"I'm tempted to go down there and find that car," he said.

"It's not your case," Duncan told him again.

"I've got some sick days saved up," said Sheehan. "Quite a few of them in fact. All of a sudden I'm feeling kind of ill. Fluey, sort of. Achy. I think some warmer weather would do me good."

19.

To get to Mikey Ferraro's house in the drab blue-collar suburb of Iselin, Benny took the Turnpike down to Exit 11 then transferred to the Parkway north for just a couple miles. Pulling in to his colleague's asphalt driveway, he took a moment to collect himself. He looked down at the stiff brown winter grass. He noticed that the shutters of the small split-level were in need of paint and that there were a couple of gaps in the row of bare shrubs around the front door, no doubt where some sad azaleas had died the season before. He took a deep breath and got out of the car.

Mikey's two kids had recently got home from school and they greeted him at the door as Uncle Benny. They wanted to show him a science project they were working on. Benny tousled their hair but told them he didn't have time just then. Mikey's wife called out from the kitchen, offering coffee and Danish. Benny politely declined. Then Mikey appeared from a hallway, wearing a New York Giants sweatshirt with the sleeves cut short. He led Benny into a small room he called the den. It had colonial style furniture with itchy looking nubby cloth upholstery. There was a football on a chair and a soccer ball on the floor. Mikey closed the door behind them and sat down lightly on the arm of a settee. "So?"

Benny chose to remain standing. "Where's my cat?" he said.

Mikey crossed his arms and pushed out his biceps. "We'll get to that. What about the job?"

"It's done," said Benny. In his own ears his voice sounded like the voice of someone whose soul had all leaked out of him.

"Tell me."

"The body's in a car compactor. Flat as Gumby by now. The gun's at the bottom of the bay."

Mikey took a moment to let that settle in. Then he said, "I didn't think you had the balls."

Benny said nothing to that.

Softening a bit, Mikey said, "Y'okay? Want a Scotch?"

Stoically, maybe even showing off a little, Benny said, "I'm fine. I don't need a drink."

Mikey looked down at the carpet and rearranged his feet. Seeming a touch embarrassed, he said, "Benny, listen, I don't doubt you, but given some of the bullshit that led up to this, the big guy says he needs some proof."

"Proof?" said Benny. He lifted an eyebrow and managed a tone of quiet but extreme bitterness. "I thought he might. Come out to the car."

The two men left the den and walked through the house with its clamor of kids fighting and the clatter of pans in the kitchen. Outside it was early dusk and a flat sky that had been drained of color was dimming moment by moment behind the rows of matching dwellings. Benny reached for the handle of the passenger door. The handcuff was still attached to the armrest and it made an almost musical tinkling sound as the door swung open. He reached in and came out with Lydia's cloth coat. He said nothing, just handed it to Mikey.

Mikey positioned his big body to hide the coat from the possibly spying eyes of his children and proceeded to examine it. There were two small, neat holes in the front left panel not far from the lapel. The material around the holes was singed from the heat of the muzzle and around the burn marks were narrow ragged haloes of crusted blood. Mikey handed back the coat and Benny tossed it into the car. Then he said, "Now where's my cat?"

Without a word, Mikey walked toward his garage, bent to grip the door handle, and yanked it open. Tasha, her taupe fur gleaming and yellow eyes hoarding the faint light, was sitting just inside the door and from her posture it seemed she'd been sitting there for days. She blinked once, meowed, and then leaped from a standing start into Benny's arms. Her body was against his ribs and he could feel her purring. Benny said, "She's fat."

"Of course she's fat," said Mikey. "You think I'm the kind of person who could starve a cat? You think my kids would let me?"

Benny said nothing, just petted Tasha, held her snugly and headed for his car.

A little tentatively, almost sheepishly, Mikey said, "No hard feelings, huh? We're cool now, right?"

In that flat and empty voice that was not his own, Benny said, "Yeah, Mikey, we're cool." But he got into his car and drove away before the other man could embrace him or even shake his hand.

Peter had mostly dried off on the bike ride home, but being pushed into the ocean by a giant thug had given sharp new focus to his inchoate and perennial worrying. In fact, as was often the case with chronic worriers, the longer he thought about the incident the more worried he got, even though the immediate danger had passed. Halfway through the cemetery, just a block away from Poorhouse Lane, he stopped his bike and told Meg they had to talk.

They sat down on a low barrier that surrounded someone's mausoleum and he said, "Honey, listen, I know you were really looking forward to a Florida vacation but, let's face it, this is not relaxing. Hiding behind the bed with a lamp in my hand in the middle of the night. Babysitting a Mafia princess. Now this Humpty Dumpty routine with some kind of Latino death squad. This isn't vacation, it's a panic attack waiting to happen. I really think we need to get out of here."

Meg said nothing, just sat there looking composed and optimistic and making Peter feel guilty for cutting short their winter getaway and cowardly for wanting to bolt.

He said, "Look, maybe we can find a place in Boca, Orlando, just some normal boring town where stuff like this would never happen."

Meg considered that as she gazed rather wistfully around the graveyard, at the sweet and compact pastel houses that were clustered along its perimeter, at the flowering trees she hadn't yet had time to learn the names of and the beckoning lanes and alleyways she hadn't yet explored. But to her husband's surprise, she sighed and said, "You're right. This is getting a little too crazy. I'll get on the computer and we'll try to make a different plan."

So they pedaled back to the Bufano house, intending, first of all, to tell Glenda they'd be leaving. This became extremely awkward when they found her curled up in the fetal pose on the living room sofa, whimpering like a small wounded animal.

On the coffee table in front of her was an empty bottle of pinot grigio and an array of damp and crumpled hankies. She was sniffling extravagantly and when Meg asked her what was wrong, all she could manage to say at first was, "He's a monster!"

"Who?" said Meg. "Who's a monster?"

"My father," said Glenda. "My Benny. Both of them." And she burst into a fresh torrent of wracking sobs.

Meg sat down on the edge of the sofa and held her bawling new friend by the shoulders but had no idea what she should say.

"My Benny, I've wanted so badly to believe he was different," Glenda sniffled on. "That he wouldn't really hurt anybody. Now he's got to kill someone. A woman, no less. A woman! And I still love him. How is that even possible? I'm supposed to sleep with a killer? Kiss him? Scratch his back? But if he doesn't kill her, he pays the price, and I'm a widow. I almost think that would be less bad...No, God forgive me, I don't think that. I don't think that even for a second. I want him back no matter what. With blood on his hands I want him back! How horrible is that? Maybe I'm just as bad as they are. Or maybe I'd never let him touch me again. Maybe I'd just be too disgusted. Jesus, I'm just so confused. Thank God you're here. If you weren't here I just don't know what I'd do."

Peter had been standing off to the side, near the sofa but not too near, just beyond the radius of Glenda's misery, his hands protectively crossed against his solar plexus. Even before his wife shot him a look from underneath her eyebrows he understood that they would not in fact be fleeing Key West that evening or probably anytime real soon. Leaving Meg to commiserate with Glenda, he quietly went upstairs to change out of his salt-crusted and rather clammy clothes.

Part 3

20.

It wasn't until dawn of the next day that Lydia finally threw away the ruined cloth coat. She and Benny, having spelled each other driving through the night, had crossed into Florida by then, and she tossed it into a dumpster behind a Cracker Barrel restaurant near St. Augustine. She'd finally warmed up enough to do without it.

When, in the parking lot of a shuttered video store a mile or so from Mikey's house, Benny had first freed her from the trunk, her teeth were chattering, her lips were white, and the rest of her skin was slightly blue. He'd handed her the cat to warm her up but she'd wanted the coat as well, bullet holes and all.

"It's got ketchup on it," Benny had warned. The condiment had come from a packet glommed from a fast-food restaurant on the ride north. "Still a little sticky."

"I want it anyway," she'd said. Surprised to find herself still alive, she saw no reason to freeze to death or to worry about a little ketchup. She'd held the cat inside the coat for the rest of New Jersey and into Delaware. She and Benny barely spoke along that stretch. They were both trying to digest the brief, bizarre drama that had played out in the junkyard.

Back in Bayway, Benny had walked Lydia to the hidden, clamorous spot where he meant to murder her. But even the way they walked there was weird and completely inappropriate for a slaying. Benny didn't push her, didn't have his gun out. He kept a hand on her back, but gently, almost as if they were on a date and he was steering her along a busy sidewalk. Lydia had been utterly calm—calm with the sort of merciful numbness that is said to settle on prey animals when they are caught in the jaws of lions or wolves, when death is a certainty but not a terror.

Benny by contrast had become a mass of tics and twitches. His left eye blinked spasmodically. His right knee locked each time he took a step. When he took the gun out and released the safety his hand was shaking and his fingers were cramped. A sudden wave of nausea hit him as he pumped the slide and heard the bullet click into place. Knowing full well that it was cowardly, he closed his eyes as he pressed the pistol's muzzle against Lydia's side. He pressed just hard enough so that he felt the texture of human flesh beneath the clothing—the sliding yield of skin, the frail resistance of a rib--and at that moment killing her became totally impossible. For several heartbeats the two of them stood there absolutely still, he with his jaw clenched and his teeth aching, she almost languid in her posture. Then Benny lowered the gun and said, "Shit, I just can't do it."

Lydia blinked at him but said nothing. The appalling atmosphere of the junkyard washed over them with its stink and noise. Finally the failed assassin, his eyes averted, said, "Here," and he handed her the pistol. The butt of it was hot from his hand, the barrel was ice cold.

Lydia's fingers accepted the weapon before her mind had quite processed that she was doing so. She had never in her life held a gun before. She looked down at it with curiosity and horror, and said, "So what the hell am I supposed to do with it? Shoot myself?"

"Or me," said Benny wearily. "Doesn't matter."

Lydia might have considered that, but only for a moment. She shook her head and said, "No way. I'm no killer."

Almost pleading, Benny said, "Look, one of us has got to go."

"You sure?"

He gave a rather spastic, helpless shrug and nodded.

Lydia said, "Well, okay, if you're sure." She calmly and deliberately raised the gun to her temple and curled her index finger around the trigger. Benny flinched and cringed in expectation of the shot but then sprang up and grabbed her by the crook of the elbow and pulled her hand away.

He found himself breathless from the momentary scuffle but Lydia was smiling. "That was a bluff," she said. "A total bluff. So I have a question for you. Why?"

"Why what?"

"Why does one of us have to go? You don't want to kill me. I don't want to kill you. You wouldn't even let me kill myself. So why does one of us have to die? Just because some bigshot says so?"

"Well, yeah. Pretty much."

"I don't buy it."

Exasperated, miserable, Benny said, "Listen, Lydia, here's how it works. If I don't do you, someone'll do me. Then they'll do you anyway. We'll both end up dead."

She put the tip of her tongue at the corner of her mouth and thought it over. "You play cards, Benny?"

"Cards?"

"It's a simple case of doubling down. Look, think of it like this. You and me, we're chips. The ante is one of us. We fold, game over, bye-bye ante. We double-down, maybe we lose both chips. But maybe we win. Or at least we get to play the game, have some action, see how it turns out. Don't you like to gamble, Benny? Don't you like the thrill of it, the rush? Come on, let's play out the hand, at least. Whaddya say?"

21.

A hundred miles behind on I-95, Special Agent Andy Sheehan had been driving alone, which was how he did most things. Juiced up on high-octane energy drinks that had been designed for younger people with less accumulated sludge in their liver and kidneys, he felt alert though irritable, and there was a dim but constant burning in his bladder. The burning had not been much relieved by stopping to pee near Fayetteville, North Carolina and it had gotten worse by the time he'd made another pit stop in Brunswick, Georgia. The simmering discomfort threatened to distract him from his musings about the case he was pursuing without permission or support.

The woman in the cloth coat—she was clearly passing inside information to Orlovsky, but where was the information coming from? Were they equal partners in the scam or was the woman just a pawn? Was Orlovsky the mastermind or was there someone else behind him and above him, pulling the strings and setting the agenda? And if the woman had in fact been kidnapped...

This last thought caught Sheehan by surprise and he tried to squelch it before it went any farther. But that was the problem with driving alone through the night, buzzed on caffeine and with an irritated urinary tract. Nerves were raw, discipline was strained, and troubling thoughts that normally could be caged by habit and routine now managed to slip through one's defenses and run their own unruly course. What if the woman had been kidnapped and had been killed by now? And what if she was no real criminal but herself a victim who'd been blackmailed or conned into making a bad decision? What if she was just trying to raise some money for a sick mother or a dying friend? Was it possible that he, Sheehan, had been wrong not to put the woman's safety ahead of his own glory-seeking, not to send an APB and have the car picked up?

This moment of doubt was only that—a moment—and it barely left a nick on the hard and polished finish of the agent's certainty. But something had registered, some tiny pinprick had marred the flawless surface, and as the dashed white lines of the highway and the ghostly silhouettes of southern pines kept streaking past, other unwanted notions were able to leak through that smallest of gateways. In some unformed and less than conscious way, the simmer in his bladder contributed to this new, grudging and unwelcome openness to questioning. The discomfort made him feel a little old; feeling old brought him perilously close to wondering if he was becoming obsolete; the merest hint at obsolescence made him feel a bit ridiculous. What the hell was he doing out here on an empty highway with his nerves frazzled and his plumbing angered in the wee hours of the morning? He pictured himself as a moving pinpoint on a giant map, a lone crusader in pursuit of...what? Of whom? Some woman who hadn't been playing by the rules. So what? The rules were often stupid, as Sheehan, an inveterate rule-breaker himself, readily admitted. And if he caught this woman rule-breaker, who would really benefit? Some banks? Some lawyers? There'd be some grandstanding about the Bureau's fight against crime, and two hours later the world would look pretty much the way it looked before, the powerful guarding their bank accounts and their mansions, outsiders scuffling around like mice along baseboards to steal a bit of cheese. And guys like Sheehan brought in as paid and well-trained pets, hungry cats let loose to catch and punish the intruders in exchange for their keep and an occasional stroke of praise. Wasn't that sort of what it came down to? For this he was trying so goddamn hard to play the hero? Maybe the younger guys—the computer cops—had it right after all. Take it a little bit easy. Let the software do the work, sleep in your own bed...

Sheehan suffered these subversive whispers across the Florida line, but finally, mercifully, they were quieted by the sanity of daybreak, and by the time the sun had topped the crowns of the palms that had begun appearing among the pines and poplars, his frayed certainty had knitted itself together once again and the fault lines were largely hidden even from himself. At a Cracker Barrel restaurant not far from St. Augustine, he stopped for grits and eggs, and then continued down the flat straight highway toward the Keys.

22.

Hoping to distract Glenda from her quandaries and her hangover, Meg had invited her out for a grocery-shopping expedition to the Publix out on the Boulevard. Buying yogurt, selecting mangoes, waiting around for quite a while as the deli person very, very slowly unwrapped and sliced turkey breast and ham—these mundane activities, Meg hoped, would foster a soothing sense of continuity, would serve as a reassuring reminder that life, even at its most stressful moments, was largely a matter, after all, of basic needs and comforting routines.

Back on Poorhouse Lane, Peter laid out silverware and napkins on the poolside table while the women prepared a luncheon platter. The three of them were passing around bowls of cole slaw and potato salad when Meg's cell phone rang. It was her policy not to answer calls at mealtimes, but when she quickly glanced over at the screen she decided she'd better pick it up.

"Hello?" she said.

"Hi. Is this Meg?" a male voice said. The voice was slightly gruff but not forceful, a rather bashful voice in fact.

"Yes."

"This is Benny. Benny Bufano. The person who—"

"Yes, I know who you are."

"Ah. How's everything down there?"

How's everything? Meg thought. Where should she start? The smashed window? The estranged wife who might be having a breakdown? The goon attack at the seawall?

"Oh," she said, "fine. Everything's fine. Nice house. Love the pool."

After she said it she looked across the table at Glenda, pointed exaggeratedly at the phone, and mouthed the words, *It's him. It's Benny.*

Glenda responded by instantly flushing a hot, congested pink, waving her arms as if desperately trying to be spotted by a rescue plane, and repeatedly mouthing back the single word *No.*

"Good," said Benny. "I'm glad it's going well." There was a slightly uncomfortable pause and then he went on. "But listen, I'm really sorry to bother you, I know this wasn't our deal, but something, um, unexpected has come up, I'm kind of in a bind, and I'm wondering if maybe I could hang out at the house for a day or two."

Meg said, "Sorry, there's some static on the line. You need to hide out at the house?"

"I didn't say hide out. I said hang out. Just till I work through a couple things. I'll try not to be in the way. I promise."

"Ah. Can you hang on a sec? Let me talk to my husband."

Meg muted the phone but before she could say a word Peter blurted out, "He wants to come *here?* Oh, perfect. Dream vacation in a desperado hideout. We can be the hostages. The human shields."

Meg said, "He said hang out. I heard hide out. It's a bad connection, I'm missing like every third word."

She unmuted the phone and went back to the call. "So, Benny, when were you thinking of coming by? Like, tomorrow?"

"Actually," he said, "more like twenty minutes. I'm just a couple miles up the Keys."

"Oh. Hold on another sec, would you?" She muted the phone again and reported the news.

Horrified, Glenda said, "Twenty minutes? No. I can't face him. I can't do it. If he's coming here, I'm bolting."

Meg said soothingly, "You'll have to face him sometime, honey. If only to see how it feels, to be sure you're really following your heart."

Peter said, "Can we please cut short the marriage counseling and decide how we can safely tell this murderer that there's no way in hell he can come to his own house?"

Glenda winced at that and Meg said, "We don't know he's a

murderer. Look, if he was going to take us hostage, you think he would've called to ask permission? He needs a place to stay. He's asking nicely. Not pushy or anything. He sounds nice. He sounds tired."

"Of course he's tired," Peter said. "You think it's easy braining people with baseball bats all day?"

Meg frowned at her husband, glanced with deep concern at Glenda, and came to an executive decision. She unmuted the phone and said, "Benny? Sure. Come by. I'm sure it'll be fine."

In a tone that was surprisingly humble, Benny said, "Thank you. Thanks for understanding. But listen, there's one more thing—"

He didn't get to finish because Peter was now frantically waving his arms and Meg asked the caller to hold on again. "Ask him if he has the fucking cat with him. Maybe there's no cat, at least."

Meg asked, and Benny said, "You know I have a cat? Yeah, I have her. I hope that's not a problem."

"No, it's fine. We'll work it out."

"Great," said Benny. "But there's one other thing—"

"Hold on," said Meg, once again distracted by Peter doing semaphore.

"Tell him about Carlos. Tell him he almost got me drowned."

To Peter, Meg said, "Honey, don't over-dramatize. It was four inches of water."

To Benny, she said, "Oh, and I think you missed a meeting with somebody named Carlos."

"Shit," said Benny. "Totally forgot. Okay, see you soon."

"Travel safe," Meg said, and she broke off the connection.

Peter sneezed at the thought of the cat and cringed at the thought of being housemates with a killer. Glenda grimaced and ran off to the guest bedroom, where she began hurriedly throwing some things into an oversized purse, preparing to run away somewhere, anywhere.

A moment later Meg walked in and tried to talk her out of it. "Are you really sure you want to do this?" she gently asked. "You tried it once before, this storming out, and where did it get you? It made you miserable, remember? You came back to try again."

Bathing suits and underwear were flying into Glenda's bag. She said, "I know, I know. But that was before—"

"Before what? Before you knew what kind of business your husband was involved in? Come on, let's be honest here. You've known it all along. Maybe you never had to really look it in the eye before. Now you do. So—you love this man or you don't. You love him in spite of everything or finally it's finished. How can you get on with your life until you know for sure?"

Glenda did not so much sit as sag onto the bed. Her shoulders dropped, her chin turned downward in a helpless pout, she looked about fourteen years old. "You're right, I know you're right. I just don't know what to do."

"For starters?" Meg said. "For starters, wash your face. Fix your hair. Get into some of those crazy shoes you like. And when your husband gets here, meet him at the door."

"At the door? I can't."

"He has no idea you're here," Meg said. "He'll be totally surprised. Don't you see, it's the perfect opportunity to know what's really in his heart. He won't have time to think, he'll just react. You'll see him clearly and you'll know. Trust me. Do this."

23.

To Benny, as it would to anyone, it felt very odd to be ringing the front doorbell of his own house as if he were an ordinary visitor.

After ringing he stood for what seemed a long moment on the wrong side of the threshold, waiting for the Kaplans, whoever they turned out to be, to let him in. Warm sun poured down; shrubbery gave off the baked smell of mid-afternoon. Benny had barely slept for something over thirty hours. His back hurt from fifteen hundred miles in the car; strangely, his feet hurt too, though he'd barely used them. At his side, Lydia was in scarcely better shape, though there was something undeniably sexy in her fatigue and disarray. Her features had softened with tiredness; the heavy-lidded eyes were somehow beckoning. Her hair had come undone at the back and hung carelessly down against her neck. Her skirt and blouse were wrinkled as though she'd made love with her clothes on. Too exhausted to stand up quite straight, she and Benny lightly leaned against each other, shoulders touching.

Glenda opened the door.

For some seconds Benny just stood there, seeing but not comprehending. He was too wrung out to feel surprise, exactly; what he felt was utter bafflement, as if he'd slipped without noticing into a different world with a different logic and different rules and different outcomes. In the real world, Glenda had left him. She'd resisted all his urging to talk, to reconcile; she'd said she was never coming back. And now in this changed world she was standing once again in the house they'd shared, the house where they'd often been happy, regal in her tall shoes, her high hair crowning the face that he had tried to draw a thousand times since she'd walked out on him but had never quite got right. He looked at her; he slightly shifted the angle of his neck to look at her some more; and his eyes welled up with tears of gratitude and joy.

Then he remembered that he had another woman with him, leaning up against him, in fact, both of them rumpled and disheveled as if from a very wild night. The first thing he said was, "Um, I can explain."

Glenda looked from Benny to Lydia, from Lydia to Benny. "No," she said, "it's wonderful!"

Benny's heart sank. Glenda was happy that he seemed to be with someone else? Had she found someone else herself? So soon? Had she forgotten him already? Weakly, he said, "Wonderful?"

"She's alive!" said Glenda. "You didn't whack her."

Benny said, "What?"

Glenda said, "And you're alive. And you're here. And you're not a murderer. I love you, Benny. I've missed you so much."

With that they fell into each other's arms and stood there petting each other's backs and nestling their teary faces against each other's necks. The cat jumped out through the car window and ran into the house. Lydia, who'd been slightly squeezed against the doorframe by the embraces of the happy couple, discreetly slipped into the shade and coolness of the living room.

When Glenda and Benny had finally finished sniffling and hugging they found Meg and Peter standing at the base of the bedroom stairs, dressed for travel, their luggage at their feet. Glenda said, "Hey, where you going?"

Rather stiffly, nervous to be in the same room as the fearsome Benny, Peter said, "We've talked it over and we really think it's time for us to go."

Meg's averted eyes suggested that she didn't entirely agree.

"No!" said Glenda. "It absolutely isn't. Everything's fine now, can't you see? Everyone's alive. Everybody's here. Stay. Enjoy Key West awhile. Let's all get to know each other better."

Peter said, "Thank you, but no. It's really better that we go."

"Go where?" said Glenda. "New York's miserable right now. Florida's packed. Where you gonna go?"

"Not sure," Peter admitted. "Maybe Boca."

From a corner of the room, all but forgotten, Lydia said, "Boca?

Yecch. I'd rather die."

Glenda said to her husband, "Benny, these people have been just wonderful to me. Please, don't let them go."

Don't let them go? thought Peter. Were they about to become hostages after all?

But Benny just shrugged and said mildly, "Glenda would like you to stay. Which means that I'd like you to stay. So, please..."

Meg looked sideways at Peter and said, "And, damn it, I'd like us to stay. I think that makes a majority. But on one condition. We're moving to the guest room. You two take the master. The honeymoon suite. *Capisce?*"

Benny and Glenda went upstairs. Lydia lay down on the living room sofa and almost instantly fell asleep. In the downstairs bedroom, Meg and Peter were unpacking again. "I can't believe you said *capisce* to him," said Peter. "Doing Mafia shtick. You trying to get us killed?"

"Benny doesn't kill people," Meg observed. "Haven't you noticed that by now?"

"He didn't kill this one particular person this one particular time. You can't extrapolate from that to say he doesn't kill anybody ever."

"Come on, he's a nice guy. Gentle."

"Gentle. Remember that story a while back about the lion biting the lion tamer's head off? The lion was gentle. Then it had a bad day. Then somebody didn't have a head."

Meg decided to let that slide and hung up a couple of sundresses in the closet.

"Plus now we've got the fucking cat," Peter resumed. "Hair balls. Dander, whatever that is."

"Honey, it's a Burmese cat."

"So?"

"Don't you know why they're so highly prized?"

"Why would any fucking cat be highly prized?"

"Because they're hypo-allergenic. One hundred per cent. Different kind of fur. Totally no problem."

"Really?"

"Really. So breathe easy, honey. Benny's not a killer. The cat is hypo-allergenic. It's all going to be fine."

24.

Beat up from the long solo drive, strung out from the supercharged caffeine and sugar drinks he'd been chugging to keep awake, Andy Sheehan crawled through the afternoon traffic and construction zones on U.S. 1, past a disheartening and seemingly endless array of pink and turquoise motels whose marquees all said No Vacancy. Since crossing the Cow Key Bridge onto the dense little island of Key West, he'd begged for a room at several places in spite of what the signs said. Desperate, he'd even flashed his badge a couple times. The tactic got him nowhere. Key Westers, unimpressed with when not actively hostile to authority, were less, not more inclined to help a Fed.

Finally, when he'd almost run out of island—almost reached the fabled Southernmost Point, ninety miles of myth and Gulf Stream from Havana—he came upon a dive that, with characteristic local humor and complete unvarnished honesty, was called the Last Resort. It was an old-style motor court, a tight cluster of cheesy and thin-walled rooms in a U-shape around a lumpy asphalt parking lot with weeds squeezing up through the cracks. It was flanked on one side by an all-night drugstore and on the other by a huge garage where they rented motor scooters. In the cubicle-sized front office sat a fat man with a greasy silver ponytail. He didn't bother looking up until Sheehan asked for a room.

"How long you want it for?"

"Not sure yet."

"All night?"

"Yeah, all night. Just not sure how many nights."

"Lemme know by noon if you want it again. Seventy bucks. Cash only."

That was it for registration. Sheehan took his key and found his room. The door to it, swollen with humidity, was stuck in its frame and needed shouldering to open. Inside there was a rug that had once been gold in color but was now stained and dimmed to a shade like the crust on too-long opened mustard. It stank of mildew. The bed had a thin mattress with a trench in the middle like a shallow grave. The bathroom floor was linoleum, scabbed and unglued at the corners where water had seeped through; the plastic shower curtain was splotched with furry black dots of mold. From the scooter place next door came the staccato racket of people starting up their nastily whining engines and trying out their blaring horns.

The odd thing was that Sheehan really liked the place. The seediness, the grit, the slow decay of long neglect; to him, it looked and smelled and sounded like police work—the kind of police work he'd been born and trained to do in the kind of world he understood. The stink and the noise and the general discomfort were strangely homey, reassuring; the misery confirmed him in his vocation, made him feel, in his way, the joy and the peace of suffering for one's art. Removing nothing but his shoes, he lay down on the bed that seemed to hum with a thousand guilty secrets and fell into a deep sleep that got him through to early evening.

On Poorhouse Lane, Benny and Glenda had had a passionate reunion and a snooze. Lydia had napped on the sofa, borrowed the guest bathroom for a shower, and changed into a rather fetching pale blue sundress generously lent by Meg; the sundress was a little snug on her, especially in the bust, and it added to her overall aspect of slightly unkempt and untapped sensuality. Peter, feeling as he often did like the odd man out, spent some time reading by the pool and then some time watching the cat perched on the kitchen counter, waiting for a chance to drink from the faucet. To his surprise and secret embarrassment he found himself playing with the cat. Not touching it, of course; just turning the water on and off to see what the cat would do. The cat got faked out several times and then it looked at Peter with its yellow eyes and meowed. Peter left the faucet running, mildly amused by the way the cat cupped water on its tongue and drank its fill without even getting its whiskers wet.

The sun went down, the light softened, and everyone got hungry. Meg suggested that they all go out for a celebratory dinner, but Benny deflected the notion, saying how nice it would be to hang around the pool and order in some pizzas. Waiting for the delivery, they all drank wine and worked at making small talk. But by the time the pizzas arrived and had been placed on the outdoor table still in their cardboard boxes, the safe chit-chat had been pretty well exhausted.

Seated, Benny graciously gestured for his guests to help themselves before reaching in for a big slice of pepperoni. Peter and Meg had gone for the vegetarian option and were just about to start eating with knife and fork when they saw their host fold his slice in half, support the drooping tip of it with an index finger, and prepare to lift it to his face, Staten Island-style. Not wanting to give offence or look too hoity-toity, they did likewise and started eating. After they'd all blistered their palates with the first hit of boiling oil and volcanic melted cheese, Benny put his slice down, dabbed his mouth on his napkin, and drank some wine. Then he said to Peter and Meg, "So, I gather from Glenda that you two basically are in the know about, let's say, my situation."

Meg nodded vaguely. Peter, worried that whatever he said would be the wrong thing, said nothing.

Benny went on. "You know more than you would know under, let's say, more normal circumstances. Is that right?"

Peter and Meg just nodded.

"Probably you know more than you wish you knew. Is that fair to say?"

Peter stayed silent. Meg hesitated, then said, "Yes and no."

Her husband kicked her under the table. She ignored the kick.

"Yes and no?"

"We didn't like knowing you were supposed to ice Lydia," said Meg. "Knowing that was kind of creepy. But we're glad to know you didn't do it. That was nice of you."

"Thank you," Benny said. "Thank you for saying that. But now we got a problem."

"Problem?" Peter managed through a pinched-down throat.

"Lydia's supposed to be dead. My boss thinks I did the job. If he finds out I didn't, if anybody sees her, I'm fucked, to put it simply. That's why, for example, we couldn't go out for dinner. But the pizza's not bad, right?"

He went back to his slice.

From the other side of the table, Lydia spoke up. "So the deal is I have to disappear. Which, frankly, I think is really pretty cool. I mean, what would I be disappearing *from?* My life before was dull, dull, dull. Then finally I have a little fun and it almost gets me killed. But if I disappear, if I just start over, then it's all fun, all adventure. I'm ready for that. I'm psyched."

"Wow," said Meg. "Disappearing. Starting fresh. It's almost like reincarnation."

Peter rolled his eyes.

"But without having to worry," Glenda put in, "about coming back as a duck or something."

"But where will you disappear to?" Meg asked.

Lydia glanced deferentially at Benny, who was just then reaching for a second slice of pizza, meatball this time.

"We're working on a plan for that," he said. "Talked about it on the ride down south. There's a few details that still need ironing out. So the main thing in the meantime is that we're all on the same page about hiding Lydia. Everybody good with that?"

25.

Later, in the privacy of the guest bedroom, Peter whispered, *"Everybody good with that?* Hell, no, I'm not. We're going to end up getting busted as accomplices or accessories or something."

"Accomplices to what?" asked Meg.

"Who knows? Nothing good."

"I think it's exciting. How many people, they go on vacation, nothing happens, it's like they never went away. Here, something is happening."

"What? What's happening? A Cosa Nostra slumber party that we're stuck in the middle of. Waiting for this little pizza-chomping Houdini to make a woman disappear."

Meg was about to reply but was pre-empted by a loud meowing at the bedroom door. She and Peter tried to ignore the squealing sound but then it came a second time and a third. Before he could stop her Meg had opened the door, and before he could dodge the contact the cat had run in and rubbed against his ankle. Peter did a little hop-step to get out of the way and the cat rubbed against his other ankle. Looking down, trying to skip backwards, he said, "How do the little fuckers always find the person who can't stand cats?"

Meg looked down also and said, "What is it, Tasha? You want a drink? Come on."

She gestured to the cat and started heading toward the kitchen but the cat just sat there looking up adoringly at Peter.

"Shit," he said. "This is so perverse."

"Maybe she sees things that people can't. Maybe she sees your aura."

"Don't start with the aura bullshit, okay?"

The cat was purring now and tracking Peter's every juke and feint so it could keep its thrumming ribcage against his leg. Finally, secretly flattered in spite of his seeming chagrin, he walked Tasha to the kitchen and watched with a smile that he hoped no one saw as she curled her tongue to drink water from the faucet.

Parked under a majestic Poinciana tree at the end of Poorhouse Lane, Andy Sheehan had watched the pizza delivery man come and go, then waited until lavender evening had become indigo night to get out of his car and have a look around.

The first thing he did was to stroll with no particular stealth toward the vehicle he'd seen receding down West 93rd St. and careening onto West End Avenue, presumably carrying away the woman he'd been tailing. He examined the outside of the car, which was entirely unremarkable. Then he produced a tiny flashlight and looked at the interior. On the floor of the back seat there were some food wrappers and coffee cups, the detritus of a long and hurried drive. On the dashboard stood one of those plastic hula girls whose hips sway and whose grass skirt moves with the motion of the car. On the passenger-side door the inside handle was missing; from the armrest dangled a pair of handcuffs. In the narrow bluish beam from the flashlight, the cuffs looked cheap and rather flimsy, not much sturdier than toys, but adequate to keep a kidnapped woman where she was.

Sheehan switched off his light and stood there in the street. From somewhere behind him a streetlamp hummed and cast a pink-orange glow; moths capered all around it, their faint and flickering shadows dappling the light. Seeing the handcuffs, the agent had felt a pang, but he couldn't quite make out what the pang was all about, and the lack of sureness rattled him. Could it be remorse that he hadn't done more to rescue the woman who'd clearly been kidnapped and might very well be dead by now? Some splinter of doubt that he'd handled the situation as a good cop should handle it? Or just frustration that possibly he'd lost the key informant in a case that could make him a hero? And why wasn't he more certain how he felt? Maybe it was just fatigue. Or loneliness. Or the heavy, hazy air of Key West that tended to blur hard edges, that took some of the snap out of brittle creeds.

In any case, he'd never been one for long bouts of introspection, and he soon turned his attention to the neat and stately house in front of him. Its deep porch was dark. Inside, random lights were on, throwing yellow parallelograms of brightness here and there through open windows. Sheehan scanned the property to find the best vantage point for peeking in; he chose a side yard that the house seemed to share with an unlit and possibly derelict shack next door. Stepping carefully over the inevitable debris of tropical gardens—the crunching tangles of fallen fronds, the slip and slide of giant rotting leaves—he made his way to a patch of shadow that offered a view into what seemed to be a downstairs bedroom.

Inside, a very ordinary-looking man of forty-five or fifty was doing what appeared to be a flailing and arrhythmic little dance that hinged his hips jerkily backwards while his shoulders asymmetrically lifted nearly to his ears. Shifting his viewpoint just a little, Sheehan saw that the man was trying to avoid contact with a cat that was slithering insistently around his ankles.

Cautiously slinking to the next haven of shadow, the agent peered into a modern gracious living room. Sleek off-white furniture was arrayed in conversational groupings. High-tech audio and video components were elegantly stacked on chrome shelves. A woman in a blue sundress was sitting on a sofa, looking at a magazine.

Sheehan's breath caught and his heart sped up when he saw her. Without doubt she was the woman in the cloth coat from New York, and yet she looked so different here. Before, her hair had been so tightly pinned as to be nearly invisible; now it dangled down across her neck and fringed along the curving line of her shoulders. Before, her face had been closed up and blank; now her eyes seemed wide and candid, her lips were slightly parted and seemed expectant, playful. In the cloth coat, her body had been indistinct, generic, but now, in the sundress that didn't quite contain her, her figure could be seen in its specificity and ripeness. She tapered from the bosom to the waistline and yet there was a hint of ampleness and comfort in her sides. Her knees were crossed and presented just a hint of dimples, like a baby's knees; the hem of the sundress lay lightly against the skin of her thighs and there seemed to be pleasure in the soft collision of fabric and flesh.

Sheehan watched her for some moments and almost admitted to himself that he was watching her now not as a cop but as a man—an unseen man standing in the dark and watching a woman bathed in a pool of lamplight who did not know she was being watched. He looked at her a furtive moment more then slunk away through the covering dimness and back to his car.

26.

At nine a.m., mid-morning in many places but quite early for Key West, there came a knock at the front door.

The knock caused a slight panic and a scramble inside the house. Despite the conversation about hiding Lydia, there'd been no discussion, still less a drill, about how this should actually be done in case there was a visitor. So now everything was confused improvisation. Lydia herself sprang up from the sofa where she'd slept, pranced barefoot toward the guest bedroom just recently vacated by Meg and Peter who'd gone to the kitchen to scare up some breakfast, and hid herself in the closet. Glenda quickly gathered up the sheet and pillow from the sofa and stuffed them into the liquor cabinet. Benny came trundling downstairs from the master suite in a blue silk bathrobe, smoothing what was left of his hair and trying to compose his features into an *everything's fine* expression. He glanced behind him to double-check the room, took a deep breath, and opened the door.

Before him stood Mel, the dirty old man who lived next door. "Benny," he said, "you're back."

"Yes, I am."

"And Glenda's back."

"Yes, she is."

"So...things are good?"

"Things are good."

Mel got the twinkle in his eye that always appeared when he was working a conversation around toward his favorite subject. "Like, *really* good?"

"Really good. But listen, Mel—"

"Even though you brought another woman home with you?"

By reflex Benny said, "No I didn't."

Mel's watery pale eyes swam and glinted in their sockets. "That's your story, you stick to it. I'll just forget I saw you coming up the walkway with a brunette, leaning all over each other and looking like you just rolled out of the sack."

"Oh, her," Benny improvised. "She was a hitch-hiker. I gave her a lift is all."

"And I'll bet she gave you one, too. Funny, I saw her go in but I never seen her leave." As he said this, Mel tried to peek around Benny's thick torso to see into the house.

Benny shifted his bulk left and right by small gradations to glut up as much of the doorway as possible. Then he said, "Listen, Mel, it's good to see you but I got a meeting I gotta get to. Is there something--?"

"Well, yeah, there is. That's why I'm here. You had a Peeping Tom last night. Course, with what you got going on in there, who could blame a guy for peeping? Anyway, I thought you'd want to know."

Benny's face instantly darkened; the top of his bald head flushed a throbbing pink. "When was this, Mel? What time?"

"Not real late. Nine-thirty, ten. Guy was parked a long time under the big tree. Then he sort of sized up the house and snuck into the side-yard. Looked in one window, just quick, then moved on to another. Living room, I think. Might've been the same window that got busted with the coconut a few nights ago. Lot of action at that window. He stood there quite a while, like he was seeing something really good."

Mel smiled at that. Benny didn't. "Wha'd he look like?"

The neighbor shrugged. "Couldn't see all that much detail. But he was tall. Seemed clean-cut, not like some neighborhood dirtbag or run of the mill pervert. Walked back to his car—"

"What kind of car? Caddy? Benz? Beemer? Was it black? Dark windows, anything like that?"

Mel got just slightly flustered at the sudden urgent questioning. "Well, I'm not real sure. But no, I think it was just, you know, an average kind of car, maybe gray or silver, something like that."

Benny allowed himself a very brief and very tentative moment of relief. He doubted anyone working for Frank Fortuna would be driving just an average car.

"Anyway," Mel went on, "he got in, took one last look and drove away. Just thought you'd want to know."

Carlos Guzman was a small, lean, natty fellow with a bifurcated pencil moustache shaped so that the two halves arced up toward his nostrils in the middle. His black hair was neatly parted. The pleats in his gray silk trousers lay perfectly flat and his linen guayabera was buttoned to the throat. Seated at his desk between two hulking bodyguards, one of whom was the brute who'd pitched Peter off the seawall, he looked somehow like a slender volume of poetry coddled between two giant bookends. For a long moment, before he said a word, he just glared at Benny with a gaze that was as cool and steady as that of an owl. The gaze wasn't an angry look but there was disapproval in it. Finally he said, "You disappointed me the other day. I thought I was dealing with a businessman."

Benny squirmed in his seat because he knew deep down that he was not a businessman, though he hoped to be one someday. He was trying to learn how. He'd put on a shirt with a very tight collar for this meeting, and even a tie. He tried to mimic Carlos's elegant manners and easy but authoritative posture, but the effort made him perspire even in the chilly air-conditioned office and he could feel his shirt growing damp along his spine. He said, "I'm sorry, Carlos. I was called out of town on a very urgent matter. A high-stress kind of thing. I just forgot about our meeting. I blew it. I'm sorry."

Carlos gave a slight nod, which seemed to be as far as he would go in accepting the apology. He said, "And now you'd like to resume our negotiations. You have such confidence that the opportunity is still available?"

In spite of himself, Benny leaned forward and put his elbows on Carlos's desk. He knew it was a sloppy pose, unbusinesslike, but he couldn't really help it, it's who he was. He said, "Actually, I wanted to see you about something altogether different. Something very pressing.

Can we talk?"

He glanced very quickly at the two bodyguards but Carlos made no gesture to dismiss them and his gaze never wandered from Benny's dampening and gradually flushing face. After a clumsy pause he cleared his throat and went on.

"I have a friend, a woman, who needs to disappear. I'm hoping you can help her get to Cuba, arrange papers so that she can stay there."

"Stay there? How long?"

"I don't know. Maybe forever. Or till she can make other plans."

"This friend, she has a passport? Money?"

"Right now she has nothing. She left home very suddenly. She can't go back. I'll cover the cost."

Carlos didn't smile at that but his moustache moved a little and something just slightly mocking came into his voice. "You will? Or your father-in-law will?"

Benny's scalp flushed a shade darker at that. "I will. This has nothing to do with him."

"Ah," said Carlos, and he paused to consider. For the first time he pulled his stare away from Benny and looked through the window of his office. The office was on the third floor of one of the harbor-front buildings Carlos owned. Below, berthed in orderly marinas, were big fishing boats and sailboats, their gleaming tuna towers and masts seeming to nod politely in greeting each other as the vessels rocked ever so slightly in the breeze.

"This woman who needs to disappear," he resumed at last. "Why?"

"I'd rather not say."

Carlos folded his hands. They were perfectly manicured and there seemed to be clear lacquer on the fingernails. "I respect your discretion," he said, "But I do not do business blind and I can not accept that answer."

Benny blinked, licked his lips, and sweated.

"She's wanted by the authorities?" Carlos asked.

"No," said Benny, which was true as far he was aware.

"A domestic situation? A jealous husband? A love affair gone wrong?"

"No. Nothing like that."

Carlos unclasped his pretty hands and lay them flat across the desk. "Benny," he said, "I don't have time to sit here playing guessing games with you. If you want my help you have to tell me why this person needs to flee."

Benny frowned and looked down at his lap. He was chagrined to see the wrinkles in his bunched up pants and the way their bottoms failed to reach the tops of his socks. He'd so badly wanted to handle this meeting well, coolly, professionally, and now he felt the last small chance of that slipping away. His voice rose in pitch though not in volume, and he weakly blurted out, "Carlos, please. She's a nice person and if she doesn't leave she'll die. That's all I can tell you. Isn't that enough?"

The neat man's face revealed nothing of whether it was enough or not. He lifted his hands from the desk, slowly bent his elbows, and lightly tapped the pads of his fingertips together. "Come again tomorrow," he said at last. "I'll think it over."

He looked toward the window once again and Benny knew the meeting was finished. Secretly, he tried to smooth the front of his trousers and to tuck his shirt in more securely before rising from his chair and heading for the door.

27.

"Oh hell," said Lydia, having tried on several bathing suits offered on loan by Glenda and Meg, none of which could quite accommodate her curves. "These just don't work for me. Anybody mind if I go topless?"

"Make yourself happy," Glenda said. Meg just shrugged and headed out to the pool with her yoga mat. Peter was already out there, reading. The cat lay contentedly on the cool flagstones in the shadow of his lounge chair, and when he thought no one was looking Peter would reach down and scratch the cat behind the ears. Every time he did it, the cat would blink its yellow eyes, throw its head back and yawn with pleasure, then nestle its skull against Peter's palm, asking to be scratched some more. When Lydia came out and removed the oversized tee shirt that she'd borrowed, Peter tried to be grown-up, almost European, and not to stare for more than a second or two.

It was a stunning late morning in Key West. The earlier haze had lifted, leaving behind a fresh-washed blue sky dotted with little teases of white cloud that shrank and vanished even as you watched. Moment to moment the sun grew warmer, the reflected heat more enveloping, caressing; the breeze came in random puffs that brought different aromas every time—sometimes the sharp brine of nearby sea, sometimes the musk of fleshy flowers stretching open for the day.

Meg finished her yoga and started doing aerobics in the pool. Lydia joined her, and the two of them stood waist-deep in the shallow end, hands braced on the bordering tiles, kicking in unison like aspiring Rockettes.

The breeze increased just slightly. From the surrounding palms came the restful and familiar sound of rattling fronds, a rhythmic scratching, like maracas. Then the sound went off the beat. A new sound—a muffled crack, then a gradually rising ripping noise, as of heavy fabric being rent—filled the air as a spent frond bent double and began with somehow tragic slowness to peel away from the supporting trunk. The dying frond creaked, paused, seemed for an instant to steady itself, and then it could be seen that among the brittle tendrils a pair of human hands were grasping and flailing and a pair of human legs were kicking and clasping, trying desperately to hold on. The frond drooped further, its angle against gravity grew more and more improbable, and finally it fell, carrying its passenger along with it. It landed on the tall dense hedge that went all around the Bufano's pool and yard, and when it hit, a man rolled forth from the wrecked foliage as though emerging from a chrysalis. He bounced off the top of the hedge, snapping small twigs as he tumbled, and came to earth at last in a loamy bed of pansies and impatiens around five feet from the pool. With impressive dexterity and presence of mind, he spun in the dirt and extracted a small-caliber revolver from the waistband of his pants as he scrambled to his feet, assumed the brace position, and shouted, "Everybody freeze!"

Peter rolled off his lounge and almost landed on the cat.

Glenda had been sucking iced tea through a straw. Through lips that were still slightly puckered, she said, "Who the fuck are you?"

The man with the gun said, "Special Agent Andrew Sheehan, FBI."

Lydia, still topless, cool water glinting on her skin, sounded unimpressed. "FBI. You're the peeper, aren't you? You think no one saw you peeping? First through the window, now up a tree. That's pathetic."

Glenda, not for nothing her father's daughter, said calmly but firmly, "You got no business here. Get out, or do we call our lawyers?"

Sheehan ignored that. To Lydia he said, "You. Put something on."

"Why? Am I making you uncomfortable?" She rounded her shoulders and leaned slightly forward, a la Marilyn Monroe. "You're the peeper. Go ahead, peep."

Sheehan tried to look away, and failed. He said, "Where's the man who kidnapped you?"

"Kidnapped me? You're crazy. No one kidnapped me. I'm here with friends."

"Your friends always handcuff you when they take you for a ride?"

"What I do for relaxation is no concern of yours. Why don't you just shimmy back up your tree and pick some coconuts?"

Meg pointed at the agent's arm and softly said, "Your elbow's bleeding. It's dripping on your pants."

The stoic Sheehan ignored her. To Lydia, he said, "What's your name?"

The bare-breasted woman all but laughed in his face. "You don't even know my name? Peeping, snooping FBI and you don't even know my name. But okay, I'm a sport, I'll help you out. Lydia Greenspan."

Sheehan said, "I'll remember it. And I think you should remember mine. I think maybe you're going to need my help some time."

"I doubt it."

"Don't. I have some pretty incriminating pictures--"

"Oh really? So you're not just a peeper but a paparazzo?"

"—of you with a crooked stock trader named Marc Orlovsky--"

"Never heard of him."

"—passing information at Grand Central."

"Grand Central? Where about a million strangers bump into each other every day. That's lame. Face it, you got nothing on me, copper."

In the next heartbeat, Lydia thought, *Copper*? Where the hell did that come from? She'd never used the term before in her whole life. Was it some vague memory of a film noir seen long ago, some cheesy women's prison flick? Or did the brash word emerge from something more mysterious and deeper, some primal badness and defiance that was finally bubbling over after thirty-seven years of being tightly lidded? In any case, something changed between her and Sheehan in the instant that the word came out. His gaze moved from her breasts to her eyes and there was a mutual recognition, a reluctant and unadmitted but powerful perceiving of kinship in the feisty and taunting look they shared. In a flash they understood that in their secret souls they were just alike, playing at virtue and seething with subversion, pretending to respectability and all the while yearning for the heat and danger and hellish pleasures of the improper and the disallowed. In that moment they moved the small but crucial distance from being simple adversaries to becoming co-conspirators in a tangled and beguiling game.

Sheehan's eyes stayed on her face now. He said, "Look, I have an idea. How about we start this conversation over?" He put the revolver back in his waistband and stood at ease. "I say I have something on you. You say I don't. Doesn't matter. You know why I came down here? I came down here because I thought you were in trouble."

"Bullshit," she said. "You came down here because it's your job."

He ignored that and went on. "I thought you were kidnapped. Maybe I was wrong about that but maybe I wasn't. Either way, you know what? I still think you're in trouble. With the law. With your so-called friends. I think maybe you and I should talk sometime."

He reached into a pocket for a business card and walked across the flower bed and the damp tiles toward the pool. He squatted down in front of Lydia, his long thighs splaying out around her face and shoulders, his torso throwing shade so that she no longer had to squint to meet his eyes. With a wet thumb and forefinger she took the card and held it by the corner. Then, on a crazy, pure, unthinking impulse, she raised her other hand and touched the FBI man's arm where it was wounded. She dabbed away a streak of blood and traced the ragged scratch with water from the pool. Sheehan felt the good sting of chlorine and a sharper sting from Lydia's touch. The contact was over in a second.

He stood up and was ready to leave. Then there came a preposterous moment when he realized he did not know how to. Glenda pointed to an entrance to the house, just beyond the small glass table. "Use the door this time," she said. "It's so much easier."

28.

"I hope you don't mind me calling like I did," said Benny.

"Nah," said Bert the Shirt, "I was happy to hear from you."

They were walking on Smathers Beach, a mile-long strip of coral nubs and knuckles thinly covered by trucked-in sand requisitioned by the Tourist Board. Every year they brought in sand before the start of tourist season, and every year it washed away, blew away, percolated down between the bits of coral and vanished. You could tell what month it was by how much sand was left.

"I just don't know who else I can talk to," Benny said.

"Yeah, I get it. It's lonely out there sometimes, what with not knowing who to trust."

"Plus my nerves are shot."

"That much I can see."

They strolled in silence for some moments, tracking the meanders of Bert's chihuahua. For Nacho, with its three-inch legs and tiny paws, walking on Smathers was mostly an erratic and largely sideways dance in which the little creature tried to spring from one small patch of sand to the next, avoiding the larger hunks of coral—boulders to the dog-- that might trip it up.

"The truth, Bert?" Benny resumed. "The truth is that I just don't know what the fuck I'm doing these days. I'm not deciding things. Things are deciding me. You know what I mean?"

"Sure, Benny, sure."

Bert was listening but he was also looking down at his feet. As Smathers lost its sand and became more reef-like, it presented a challenge to his balance, with treacherous unsuspected humps and slick places where the slope increased with no warning. But the old man had walked a dog there every day for as long as he could remember, and he wasn't about to stop just because it got a little dicier from year to year.

"Like with this woman, this Lydia," Benny said. "It was never my idea to whack her, never my decision. But it wasn't really my decision *not* to, either. I mean, it wasn't a decision at all. It's just that I couldn't do it."

"And you should never'a been asked to," Bert responded. "That's bullshit. Back in the day, our people would never clip a woman. Ruin her life, maybe. Kill her husband, her father, take away her livelihood, burn down her house. But shoot a woman point blank, bang, you're dead— no, that never would have happened."

Benny started to say something, held back, and for a moment just looked down with dismay at the fancy, thin-soled shoes he'd worn to his meeting with Carlos in hopes of looking like a businessman. They were scratched and scuffed now, covered in fine coral dust the color of bone. When he spoke again, it was in the hushed tone of a confession. "But you know what, Bert? I can't really take this high road bullshit and say I didn't do the job because it was a woman. Even if it had been a guy I couldn't've pulled that trigger. I couldn't have. No way I could've known that for sure before. But now I know I couldn't've done it."

They walked. The dog danced ahead and deposited a few drops of urine on a volleyball that had rolled away. Bert weakly kicked it back toward the people who'd been playing with it, and then he said simply and finally to his companion, "You don't belong in this life, Benny."

"You think I don't know that? So how the hell do I get out?"

The old man shook his head. "No idea. But at least you're thinking about it before ya got blood on your hands. You're way ahead of where I was at your age."

Benny gave a quick unhappy laugh. "So I guess that's the good news. But meanwhile I gotta get this woman stashed someplace."

"You have a plan for that?"

Benny told him.

Bert listened with his hand on his chin and his head cocked at a sagacious angle, then he said, "The Cuba part I like. The Cuba part's a natural. Involving Carlos, that I'm not so sure about."

"Who else could I have asked?"

"That's a point. No one that I know of. S'okay, it's Carlos. How well do you know him?"

"Not very," Benny admitted. "You know, from around town, mutual acquaintances. I went to him a month or so ago about this other idea I had—"

"Other idea?"

Benny got shy. "Doesn't matter. Probably dumb. Probably impossible. A business thing. Legit. Anyway, I was just looking to rent a place from him. I thought he might be someone I could talk to, you know, a businessman but not a stiff, someone who'd get it that I've never bothered with banks or credit checks or any of that bullshit."

"Someone legit but not too legit," Bert said.

"Yeah, something like that."

"Well, I guess that pretty much sums up Carlos. Complicated guy. Reminds me a little of a younger, smarter, Cuban version of your father-in-law. Mix of criminal and, whaddyacallit, entrepreneur. Except that with Fortuna it's like ninety-eight percent thug and two percent citizen. With Carlos it's more like fifty-fifty. Makes him a lot harder to read. You paying him for his help?"

"He hasn't agreed to help yet," Benny pointed out. "But yeah, if he helps, it'll be for money."

"Good. Keep it simple. Cut and dried. Fee for service. None of this vague owing a favor bullshit."

Benny nodded.

"And one other thing," Bert said. "If you throw in with Carlos, have a backup plan."

"Backup plan?"

Bert said nothing for some seconds. He was gazing off toward the horizon, a hazy blue-green seam where the sea curved away and the sky seemed to lean down over it like a mother tucking in a child. "Ya know, in case he doesn't one hundred percent exactly fulfill his half of the bargain. In other words, like if he decides to take your money and fuck you right up the ass."

Benny swallowed and kicked a piece of coral with his dusty shoes. He said, "So, like, what kind of backup plan?"

"I have no idea," said Bert the Shirt. "Just have one."

29.

"So honey, how was your day?"

"Christ," said Benny, "I could use a martini."

They were standing in the doorway of their house, just disengaging from a welcome-home hug. Glenda had fixed her hair the way her husband liked it best, swept up from her forehead and her temples, piled and twirled on top. She'd changed into a loose-fitting, languorous shift in shades of purple and magenta. She said, "They're already made. In the freezer so they won't get watery."

Benny clutched both his wife's hands when she said that and his eyes briefly welled up with tears of gratitude. He vaguely wondered what the hell was going on with him. Before the last couple days, he hadn't cried in fifteen, maybe twenty years, and suddenly everything was making him weepy; he teared up with thankfulness just because his wife had thought to make him a drink. It was like he was a leather jacket that had been turned inside out so that the soft side where the meat and nerves and blood had been was finally exposed. He said to Glenda, "Baby, please, don't ever leave me again."

She kissed him on the cheek and led him through the kitchen and out to the shady table by the pool. When they'd clinked glasses and sipped the first stinging bit of gin, Glenda said, "So, you met with Carlos? He'll help?"

"He'll tell me tomorrow. Meanwhile he made me feel like a slob."

"You're not a slob, honey."

"This guy, every hair's in place. Nothing's wrinkled. He doesn't sweat. I've never seen anyone like that. He looks like a goddamn anchorman." He nipped at his martini and went on. "I called Bert afterward. Needed to talk. Bert doesn't really trust him. But enough about me. How are you? What's been going on around here?"

Glenda looked down at the table. She fished the toothpick out of her martini glass and nibbled on an olive. Cherishing the sweet romantic moment, not wanting to cloud it over, she stroked the back of Benny's hand before saying, "Well, the FBI was here."

"*What?*"

"Not the whole FBI. One guy. He fell out of a tree."

"A tree?"

"A palm. A frond let go. He was sort of wrapped up inside it, sort of like a cannoli. He fell over there." She pointed to the flower bed where some pansies and impatiens were trying to recover from being squashed. "Turns out he was the peeper from last night."

Benny had to admit to himself that this was relatively good news. Better the Feds than one of his former buddies from the crew. "Okay," he said, "a cop falls out of a tree. Then what?"

"He went over to Lydia. She didn't have a top on."

"No top?"

Discreetly lowering her voice, Glenda said, "She's got big boobs. We didn't have anything that fit her."

"All right, all right, forget about the boobs. What happened?"

"He talked to her. Said she was in trouble. Said she'd need him sometime. Tried to scare her. But she didn't scare."

Benny sipped some gin. "You sure?" He asked it quietly but it was a question of some importance. If Lydia got scared enough to turn under the protection of the FBI, there was every chance that she could save her skin and maybe not even do jail time. She might even bring down Frank Fortuna. But in the meantime Benny would definitely, without a doubt, be iced.

"I'm pretty sure," said Glenda. "She didn't rattle. She let him talk and then she told him off."

Benny nodded and considered. He mostly trusted Lydia. She was reckless and she had a death wish but all in all he believed she was solid. And besides, back in the New Jersey junkyard, she and Benny had each had the chance to kill the other and both had taken a pass. How likely was it that she'd sell him down the river now?

Then Glenda very softly resumed, "But—"

"But what?"

"But something's going on between those two. The way he looked at her."

"Well, sure, she's got big boobs and she didn't have a top on."

"But that's the thing," said Glenda. "That's not where he was looking. I mean, he checked them out, of course he did, but then they just locked eyeballs. Really stared. For a long time. They stared so hard that even though no one moved it seemed like their faces were getting closer and closer together. You know what it was like? It was like a scene in an R-rated movie, the scene where first it's the guy's face, then it's the girl's face, then it's the guy's face, then it's the girl's face, then they make you wait, then everybody parts their lips and in the next second they're chewing on each other's tongues and tearing each other's clothes off."

Benny said, "I think maybe you're exaggerating."

"No, I'm really not," said Glenda. "Those two have some kind of hot game going on and I don't think it's cops-and-robbers."

30.

In the guest bedroom, Peter was sitting in a wicker chair. The cat was on his lap and he was scratching it behind the ears. This rhythmic scratching had in recent hours become a sort of nervous tic with Peter, and it already felt so natural that it would have been hard for him to remember what he did to skim off nervous tension before the cat had slinked into his life.

Meg was half-reclining on the bed, her head propped on a stack of pillows. Lydia was luxuriously arrayed on a *chaise longue*, her ankles crossed, the oversized tee shirt draping loosely over the tops of her slightly sunburned thighs. In a breathy and softly rapturous alto voice she was telling Meg about the galvanizing strangeness of the look she'd shared with Andy Sheehan. "I've never felt anything like it in my life. It was more than just excitement. It was...I don't know, this'll sound corny...it was like destiny. Compulsion. What's that word people use when they're wildly, crazily attracted to someone and it takes them over, they know they can't escape from it? Thrall. That's it. I met his eyes and I was enthralled. You ever look at a man and feel that way?"

Peter quickly said to his wife, "If it's not about me, don't say so. I'm insecure enough."

Meg said nothing, but it really didn't matter. Lydia in that moment would have had a tough time believing that anyone else had ever truly felt what she was feeling.

"The bond," she went on. "How do people feel a bond like that in a matter of seconds? I mean, we were sparring, dissing each other, being total enemies. And at the same exact time there's this *ka-POW* thing going on, like we've been lovers all our lives and were just waiting to actually meet."

"Maybe you've met before," Meg said. "In past lives, I mean. Maybe you're both old souls."

Peter said, "Can we please not start with the old souls bullshit?"

Ignoring the comment, Lydia said, "Yeah, but with old souls everyone imagines they were someone really good before. Gandhi. Mother Teresa. Buddha. This is just the opposite. I looked at him and I saw bad. And I know that's what he was seeing when he looked at me."

"You're not bad," Meg said soothingly.

"Yes I am. Look, I don't mean evil. I'm nice. I keep my word. But I'm bad. And so's he. Outlaw bad. Rule-breaker bad. Don't-mess-with-me bad. If you were bad too, you'd know exactly what I mean."

Meg had no reply to that. Peter stroked the purring cat. Lydia squirmed on her *chaise.* She seemed to find it impossible to keep her ankles from crossing and uncrossing. From somewhere inside her commodious shirt she produced the business card that Sheehan had given her. She held it by the corner, as though for fear that the very cardboard might singe her skin. "I have to see him," she said. "I have to go to him."

Peter said, "I hate to be the one to throw cold water, but you're in hiding, remember? That's the deal."

Meg said, "You could probably sneak out through the window."

"Sure," said Peter, "isn't that what windows are for? Coconuts in, fugitives out."

Lydia said, "No, I wouldn't sneak. That's not me. I'll talk to Benny, tell him this is just something that I have to do."

"Great," said Peter. "Just tell Benny the Mafioso that you feel this sudden irresistible attraction to the FBI. I'm sure he'll be very supportive."

"He'll understand," said Lydia. "Benny and me, after what we've been through together, we know each other pretty well."

"Of course," said Peter. "Probably you were old souls together too. Maybe he whacked you in a past life."

"He trusts me," Lydia said. "If I tell him I won't turn, he'll believe me."

Peter pointed vaguely through the window at the streets beyond. "And what if the wrong person sees you out there? If the wrong person sees you, Benny's old soul is going to need a new ass, because his current one is toast."

"And so's mine," countered Lydia. "Look, it's not a risk-free world."

"I've noticed."

"So liberating to accept that," Meg put in.

"He'd be absolutely crazy to let you do this," Peter said, still fondling the cat.

31.

That evening they were four at dinner.

Glenda ordered in Chinese, and when the food arrived in hot brown bags Meg and Peter had at first, by long habit, reached for the flat wooden chopsticks in their sanitary paper wrappers. But when they saw that their hostess had laid out forks and knives they politely changed to Western utensils. Peter secretly admitted that he had not enjoyed Kung Pao chicken this much in years, without having to worry about peanuts and bits of red pepper tumbling off his chopstick before getting to his face. The sesame noodles could actually be twirled and delivered to one's mouth in a tidy packet rather than as a chin-tickling mess of dangling strands. Beer was swigged directly from the bottle, rice was spooned straight from the white containers with the thin metal handles. In all, it was a pleasant and convivial family-style meal, at least until the crisis of the final dumpling.

Slightly deflated and no longer steaming, it sat alone on the plate when Benny and Peter, seated diagonally across from one another at the outdoor table, reached for it at the exact same moment. The tines of their forks touched as in some lilliputian sword fight but then both men instantly pulled back. Benny, as the host, motioned politely for his guest to take the morsel. "Please," he said. "Have it."

"No," said Peter, "it's yours."

"Really. Go ahead."

He gestured for Peter to take the dumpling but Peter didn't do it. He couldn't do it, couldn't get his fork to go so close to where Benny's fork had just been stabbing. Covering up, he said he really wasn't hungry anymore.

Benny looked sad when Peter said that. He'd heard more than self-denial or simple deference in the statement. Gently putting down his own utensil, he said to Peter, "Are you really that afraid of me?"

Disarmed by the directness of the question, Peter gave a nervous little laugh that briefly interrupted his breathing and gave him the hiccups. "No. Well. Um, yes. *H'cup.*"

"Thank you for admitting it. It hurts my feelings, but thank you. But why, Peter? Have I ever done anything to do? Ever threatened you?"

Peter shook his head and hiccupped.

"You think I'm a violent person? You think I'll just blow up sometime?"

Peter did not know what to say. Trying to help out, Meg said, "It's just because you're Mafia."

Benny nodded sorrowfully. "Okay. Mafia. But what's Mafia? It's just a word."

"Right," said Meg. "A scary word."

Peter hiccupped. This time it was a loud, two-note hiccup, a bit like a low-pitched hee-haw.

Mostly to himself, Benny said, "I hate it that people are afraid of me. I'm supposed to get off on it but I hate it."

There was a silence broken only by the rasp of crickets and the occasional half-stifled sound from Peter's gullet. Then Glenda said, "Would anyone like a fortune cookie and some orange wedges?"

Before anyone could answer, Benny abruptly stood up from the table. The movement was not threatening but there was both frustration and resolve in it. Mopping his lips on a napkin, he said to his guests, "Come with me a minute, please. Don't be afraid. There's something I want to show you."

Without another word he led the way into the house and through the living room and up the stairway to the master suite. To Meg and Peter it felt quite strange to be there again; it was like returning to a place they'd lived in long ago, except that they'd lived there a mere two days before. They'd first known that bedroom as nothing more than an anonymous chamber owned by strangers, a place to have a vacation. They'd made love in that very bed then hidden behind it poised to throw things when Glenda showed up in the middle of the night. Now they were back to being visitors. It just felt odd. What was so peculiar was that the room itself hadn't changed at all. It was the same exact same room it had always been, but then again it wasn't.

Benny had switched on a light and stood now between the foot of the bed and the closed door of his closet. Somewhat theatrically, he tried to turn the doorknob. "Locked," he said. "But I'm guessing you noticed that."

Meg said nothing. Peter covered his mouth with his fist and tried to smother a hiccup.

"Hey, it's okay," Benny said. "Human nature. Strange house, locked closet. Who wouldn't be curious?"

"*I'm* curious," said Glenda, who had trailed the group and now was leaning in the bedroom doorway. To Peter and Meg, she said, "He never even lets me see what's in there."

"You least of all," said her husband, before returning his attention to his guests. "S'okay. Strange house, locked closet. Could be anything, right? Then you hear this strange word, this scary word. Mafia. So then what do you think? Guns? Clubs? Briefcases stuffed with cash? Come on, Peter, talk to me. What do you think is in the closet?"

"I have no idea," he stammered.

Benny paused then said, "Well, I'm gonna show you."

Peter felt a sudden clench of panic that instantly cured him of his hiccups. He didn't want to know Benny's secrets. He felt in some inchoate way that knowing Benny's secrets would only mire him more deeply in a situation he'd never wanted to be in. Weakly, he said, "You really don't have to."

"Yeah, I do," said Benny. "I do have to. I'm tired of hiding what's inside me, tired of worrying what if people found out. There's a time to come clean, and I think this is it."

Without taking his eyes off his guests he sidled over to his nightstand. He pulled open a drawer that seemed to have a false back; reaching past the divider he came out with a key. As he stepped back toward the closet there was a silent, wavelike movement in the room, the women leaning closer, Peter easing back by barely visible degrees.

Benny slipped the key into the lock and turned the doorknob. At first all that could be seen were some shirts and jackets arrayed on hangers. Then he switched on a light and stepped aside.

At the back of the closet stood a large wooden easel, and on the easel was a big sketch pad, and on the page to which the pad was opened was a portrait, done in charcoal and pastels, of Glenda. The lines of the portrait were sinuous and soft, not a hard edge anywhere, the colors pale and almost melting. The eyes were slightly turned down, rather bashfully; the mouth was halfway to a smile but seemed to hold a quiet sorrow, too. For a moment Meg and Peter and Glenda all stared at the picture and no one seemed to breathe.

Finally Benny said, "This is what I do when no one's watching. This is what I do when I'm alone. Mafia tough guy makes pictures and hides them in a closet. If anybody wants to laugh, go 'head, I'm okay with that."

No one laughed, and Benny, emboldened or just compelled to continue with his self-exposure, stepped into the closet and started flipping pages of the pad. There were images of Glenda in pencil, in ink, in crayon. There were tender, caressing drawings of trees, of flowers, of the cat. "No idea if these are any good," he said. "I never had any lessons. I regret that. But could you imagine me walking into art school? Scaring people? Ridiculous, right?"

He gestured toward a shelf where dozens of other sketch pads were stacked. To Glenda he said, "Worked on these day and night after you walked out on me. Didn't know what else to do. Drawing, it almost made me happy. Distracted me, at least. Then I started letting myself wonder if maybe this was something I could be good at, something I could do. Something other than being a dumb goombah. Something that would make you proud of me, baby."

"I am proud of you, Benny."

He instantly and secretly teared up at the words but he couldn't quite accept them. "Nah, I haven't earned that, I ain't done nothing to deserve it. I was hoping to open a gallery. You know, see if anyone liked this stuff, if anyone would buy it. That's what I was talking to Carlos about, renting a place. I wanted it to be a big surprise. Well, I guess I blew it."

A moment passed and Benny seemed to get shy again. He switched off the closet light and said, "Okay, show's over. But Peter, lemme ask you something. You still afraid of me?"

Part 4

32.

At a corner of the parking lot at the Last Resort, there was a small fenced area that once had been a garden. Hibiscus hedges had ringed it; passion vines had wound among and softened the ugly metal rhomboids of the chain-link fence. Those civilizing touches had vanished long ago, and the former refuge was now just a scruffy patch of rough grass intermixed with spiky weeds and broken glass that gave off fractured reflections from the neon signs of the surrounding businesses. Stomped cigarette butts and crushed and faded beer cans were strewn here and there; from nearby lanes and alleys a sporadic cacophony of scooter engines and drunken laughs and shrill arguments warped the air. This was the Key West that upscale tourists seldom saw, the Key West of flaking paint and busted furniture, of drifters, junkies, petty criminals, and it suited Andy Sheehan just fine.

To Lydia Greenspan's slight surprise, the tawdry neighborhood appealed to her as well. She found it not so much sinister as indifferent, unapologetic. From the moment she'd stepped out of the taxi in front of the motel, she'd felt somehow unburdened, free. There was a bracing, bristly texture to the neighborhood, an all-encompassing roughness, as though the entire precinct had been gone over with very coarse sandpaper and then left as it was. When Sheehan had met her at the motel entrance and led her to the ruined garden to talk, even the chairs they sat on were rough. The chairs were made of interwoven bands of plastic that had grown brittle and grizzled in the sun; the strands scratched at the backs of Lydia's legs as she sat there, making her uncommonly aware of her skin.

Sheehan, characteristically, had begun the conversation with a taunt. "So," he said. "You've decided to come over to the winning side."

"I never said that. I said I was coming to offer you a deal."

The agent's response to that was a slight smile and a soft but utterly confident laugh. "Lydia," he began...but then he paused. It was the first time he had spoken her name, and he was shaken to realize that the feel of it burned his mouth like a too-big gulp of whiskey. "Lydia," he said again, "here's something you don't seem to understand. You don't offer the FBI a deal. The FBI offers you a deal. Maybe."

"And here's something *you* don't seem to understand," she countered. "I'm not offering the FBI anything. What I'm offering, I'm offering to you. As a private citizen. As a man."

There was something in her eyes that made Sheehan squirm in his raspy chair so that the coruscating plastic tugged at his shirt and pants. "Go ahead."

"So here's the deal. I'm going to tell you absolutely everything you want to know about my little escapade in the stock market. And you're going to swear on your mother that you will never, ever use the information."

Sheehan came out with another brief laugh, but it wasn't quite as confident this time. He felt that the conversation was somehow getting away from him, that at some point he'd lost momentum and control and he didn't know quite when. "And why would I even consider a deal like that?"

"Oh," said Lydia casually, "I could think of a few reasons. First, it's the only deal I'm offering. Take a pass on it and you'll find out nothing."

"Don't be too sure of that," the agent said. "Finding stuff out is what I do."

"Right. I get that. You want to be the smart guy, the first to know, the guy who figures all the angles and puts it all together. But why? So you can tell your bosses and get a pat on the head and maybe even get your name in the paper for a day or two?"

Sheehan let that pass and they just eyed each other for a moment. Somewhere the sound of a siren was rising and falling. From inside an anonymous motel room came a propulsive creaking of bedsprings. Exhaust fumes from unmufflered scooters mixed with the overripe musk of browning flowers and made the air narcotic and thick.

"But okay," Lydia went on, "here's another reason. If you don't take the deal, I can promise you you'll never see me again. Would that bother you at all, Sheehan?"

She leaned just slightly toward him as she said this. He imagined he could smell her hair. He remembered her bare shoulders, the teasing, goading way she rounded them. He dimly understood that the question she'd asked was the most dangerous of questions and that if he answered it at all he was already well on his way to being finished as a cop. He heard himself say softly, "Yeah, it would."

Lydia leaned back, let her rough chair scratch at her. She smoothed her lap and her hands lingered on the tops of her thighs. "It would bother me, too," she said. "So let's talk about what might happen if you do take the deal."

Sheehan stared at her and found himself mimicking her posture. His hands were on his legs and he distinctly felt the outline of each finger as it pressed down on his flesh.

"If you take the deal," she went on, "I think what might happen is that you'd go to that liquor store across the street and buy us a pint of bourbon. Then maybe we'll sit here drinking it, taking turns from the bottle, just looking at each other. Then I think you might take me to your room and we'll see if things work out as fabulous as I think they will. What do you say, Sheehan? Deal?"

33.

Later, her head on his chest and their torsos forming a kind of arch above the valley in the middle of the sagging bed, Lydia was saying, "The thing is, the scam was just so simple. I can't believe there aren't other people pulling the same thing."

"Probably there are," said Sheehan, with a bland acceptance that surprised him. "So tell me."

She lifted up on an elbow and kissed his shoulder before continuing. "I was recruited into it by an old friend," she said, "a guy who's a paralegal at a firm that handles mergers. Big mergers. The kind of deals that move the market. Takeover targets go up twenty, forty, sixty percent as soon as word gets out. Attorneys at that firm can't have any contact with brokers. Closely watched by the SEC, and if there's anything fishy, probably by you guys too."

"Definitely by us," the agent put in, but even as he said *us* he noticed with a pang that he didn't quite feel like part of the Bureau anymore. He still had his badge; he still had his gun. But a sense of separation, of dereliction had already started to settle in. It was an empty feeling but not necessarily a bad one; it felt less like a betrayal than like a difficult but honest goodbye that had been simmering for many months.

"There's a log of every phone call, every email," Lydia went on. "But that's for the attorneys. Who cares if some lowly paralegal who happens to have access to the files has lunch now and then with another lowly paralegal whose firm is in an altogether different business?"

"So that's where you come in? The second paralegal?"

"Right. Librarian for a boring firm that does estates and trusts. Nothing whatsoever to do with Wall Street. So I get the tip, pass it to Orlovsky. Orlovsky does some quick-and-dirty research to cover his ass, make it look like he's playing fair. He executes a few big trades, looks smart, makes a bunch of money. Easy as pie."

"So Orlovsky's the linchpin?"

"That's what I thought, until I made the mistake of asking for more money. Then I found out there's a very nasty guy behind Orlovsky who's forcing him to run the scam. A big client who lost a ton of dough in the downturn a few years ago and wants to make it all back in a hurry."

"Who's the client?"

Lydia leaned down and nuzzled Sheehan's neck. "Why's it matter now? You can't use the information. You swore."

"I want to know."

"You're just teasing yourself."

"No, you're teasing me. And you said you'd tell me everything. Who's the client?"

She stroked his arm, traced out a vein that wound from his wrist to his elbow.

"Who's the client?" he said again.

"Okay," she sighed. "A mobster named Fortuna."

"Frank Fortuna!" Sheehan said, sitting up so quickly that he bumped Lydia's head with his chin. "Shit! I've wanted him for years."

"And you almost had him. Too bad you're a friend of the family now."

"Excuse me?"

"The people I'm staying with, Glenda and Benny, that's Fortuna's daughter and son-in-law. Benny was supposed to kill me because Fortuna got it in his head that I was going to turn. But he didn't kill me, and we're buddies now. The wife too. And I don't rat out my buddies. That's why you can't have Fortuna. He's still Glenda's father."

"But he's a really awful guy," said Sheehan, something almost pleading in his voice.

"You're telling me? But look, he thinks I'm dead. If he finds out I'm not, he kills Benny. No way I can let that happen."

146

Sheehan scratched his stomach for a moment and thought it over. "You and Benny," he said, "I could get you both into the Program."

"Witness Protection?" Lydia said. "You mean where you get a new face and a new name and you have no idea who you are and you're dependent on the whims of the Feds for the rest of your life? No thank you. I have a different idea."

"Which is?"

She hesitated. "You're still sworn to secrecy. Agreed?"

Grudgingly he accepted the condition.

"Cuba. I'm hoping to disappear there in a day or two."

Sheehan said nothing to that and he hoped it didn't show that he winced. But he felt slightly dizzied, as though the walls and floor had suddenly shifted. Over the past twenty-four hours he'd been gradually surrendering his certainties to the warm haze of Key West and his unruly desire for this subversive and compelling woman, and now she was vanishing to Cuba? Just like that? Sending him back, alone, to the life and purpose he was used to, but which, by anguished and half-conscious increments, he'd already begun renouncing? He worked at getting his mind around it, and meanwhile Lydia let her body slink down a little farther toward the trough in the middle of the bed so that it was pressed more firmly against his.

As if reading his thoughts, she said, "Maybe you'd like to disappear with me."

The notion was so intoxicatingly outré that at first Sheehan could only bring forth a nervous laugh. "Lydia, I have a job."

"You're not acting like you do."

"Look, I have things I'm in the middle of, things I haven't finished."

Lydia shrugged. The shrug raked her skin against his. "Being in the middle of things, that's life. It's never a convenient time to change."

"I can't quit now," he said, in the somewhat strangled voice of a person trying to convince himself. "Not just yet. I have a pension coming up."

"When?"

"Six months. Wait for me. Wait for me in Cuba."

She touched his chest, toyed with a little whorl of hair. "I don't make promises I'm not sure I can keep. Six months is a long time, Sheehan."

He tried to visualize six months, pictured a calendar, a bland parade of nights and mornings, a succession of coffee shop meals, a flickering of office lights turned off and office lights turned on again. The images gave him a pang of despair but also a fresh hunger for the moment and for Lydia. "Six months without you would be hell," he said, "but maybe I can persuade you the wait would be worthwhile."

He let himself sink down into the hollow of the bed and took her in his arms.

34.

Benny's meeting with Carlos Guzman was scheduled for ten a.m. next morning, and when Lydia still had not come home by nine-fifteen he was almost starting to think that she had sold him out.

Meg, for one, refused to believe it. "She wouldn't do that," she insisted, as the four of them sat rather gloomily around the breakfast table, poking without appetite at slabs of mango and papaya. "It's a karma thing. You saved her life. She's not going to turn around and..."

She paused out of delicacy, and Benny finished the thought for her. "Get me killed? I don't know. Why wouldn't she? I mean, everything's been so intense, so sped up, it feels like we're old friends and all of that. But think about it. How long we know each other? Three days? Four? And it's not like I did anything wonderful for her. All I did was not kill her. But I grabbed her. I scared the crap out of her. Why would she think she owes me anything?"

"She owes you plenty," Glenda said. "It's not just that you didn't ice her, it's that you're helping her get out of this mess she made for herself. You're helping her start a whole new life."

"In Cuba?" Benny said. "With dicey papers? Without friends? Nah, the Feds can offer her a better deal. That's what's unfair about this game. The Feds can always offer a better deal if they want to."

Rather to his own surprise Peter spoke up then. "It's not about the deal," he said, with a seeming assurance that no one at the table had heard from him before, and without quite realizing that his convoluted logic was borrowed straight from Bert the Shirt. "She'll do the right thing because she'll do the right thing. And she'll do the right thing because she's bad. Or thinks she is."

Glenda said, "I'm not quite sure I follow that."

The cat was on Peter's lap and he lifted it off before continuing. It looked at Peter reproachfully as he gently placed it on the floor.

"I'm not quite sure I understand it either," he went on. "But look, ever since I got here I've been misjudging people. Benny, you I thought—no offense, okay?—"

149

"Go on."

"I thought you were just a knee-breaker, a brute. Glenda...let's just say I sold you short, too. Why? Why did I keep getting it wrong? I think it's because you guys play by rules I'm just not used to. And because they're different rules, I didn't understand that they were rules at all. Does that make sense?"

"Maybe in a Zen *koan* kind of way," said Meg.

"So now here's Lydia," Peter said, "always trying so hard to convince herself that she's bad. But what I finally figured out is that being bad, or thinking you are, it takes a lot of work. I mean, if you're good—or imagine you are--you don't really have to make that many hard decisions. You do what's expected. You follow the rules that almost everybody follows."

"Right," said Benny. "You're just a solid citizen."

"Exactly," Peter said. "But if you see yourself as bad, all you have is your own code, nothing else. That's your law. It goes deep. It's who you are."

"Sometimes it's who you're stuck with being," Benny said.

"So why'd you let Lydia go to meet the Fed?" Peter asked him, then answered it himself. "You let her go because your code says that if a friend gives her word, you honor that. And *her* code says you don't screw a friend who trusted you. That's why she'll be back. *Quod erat demonstrandum.*"

"I didn't quite follow that very last part," Glenda said.

Then there was a knock on the front door. Benny sprang up to answer it and he soon came back with Lydia and Sheehan in tow. Their hair was damp, they had a glow about them, and they were holding hands. Lydia started to apologize about staying away so long, but Benny cut her short, saying it was all okay and asking her if she was still onboard.

"Absolutely," she said.

"What about him?" asked Benny, pointing sideways at Sheehan. It felt weird to have an FBI agent standing in his kitchen holding hands with a suspect and he couldn't quite get himself to address the man directly.

But Sheehan spoke up for himself. "I'm here to help."

"Help?" said Glenda. "Yesterday you were falling out of trees and pointing guns at people."

"That was then," he said, in a tone that was disarmingly mild, almost contrite. "Lydia and me, we have an understanding now."

"So lemme get this right," said Benny. "Yesterday you were a Fed and today you're not a Fed?"

It was a profoundly disorienting question but the tall man tried to answer honestly. "I'm still on the payroll, okay? But I'm not on a case. I'm reporting to no one. Call it vacation."

"Weird vacations in this town," said Peter.

Glenda was skeptical. "We got enough problems here as it is. I just don't see why the hell we should trust you."

The statement hung in the air a moment. People shuffled their feet in discomfort. Then Meg spoke up. "I think we can trust him. It's like Peter said. We can trust him because he's bad."

Sheehan's face showed nothing but his first reaction to that was inwardly to bristle. Bad? Him? The altar boy? The cop? The occasional hero? He considered the notion for a moment. Then he tried to dismiss it, but by then it had seeped into him like a stain spreading through muslin. Finally he almost smiled. "You can trust me," was all he said.

Benny straightened up his clothes and headed to his meeting.

35.

He was back in an hour, and he came home to an odd scene that was somewhere between a retro pool party and a swim-day outing at a lunatic asylum. Glenda, Lydia, and Sheehan were standing in the pool playing some mongrel version of volleyball and water polo. They'd found an old striped beach ball and improvised a net with two chairs and a clothesline. Sheehan, wiry and strong but pasty white everyplace except his forearms, played both sides of the net except now and then when he would tuck the ball and dive underwater with it, most likely so he could grab a feel of Lydia beneath the roiled surface. Meanwhile, Peter was rolling around under lounge chairs and at the bases of shrubs, holding a rubber mouse by the tail and yanking it away as Tasha tried to pounce on it. Meg was standing on her head in a shady corner of the yard, using her thumbs to alternately pinch her nostrils so she could inhale through one and exhale through the other. A soft two-note wheezing escaped her as she did this and she was murmuring something in Sanskrit.

Amid all the frolicking, it was some moments before anyone noticed Benny standing there in his hard, thin shoes and his dress shirt streaked with sweat along the backbone and his now-loosened tie still chafing against his throbbing neck. When Glenda finally spotted him she put down the beach ball and called out, "How'd it go, honey?"

Everything stopped in anticipation of the answer. Peter sat up on the pool apron, the toy mouse clutched in his fist. Meg gracefully descended to a kneeling position on her mat.

Benny said, "Went well," and a silent sigh, a collective relaxation of the shoulders went through the ill-assorted little group.

But then his face darkened and he slowly sat down in a chair. The slowness of the movement suggested not defeat, exactly, but bewilderment, the burden of a crucial riddle perhaps misunderstood. "Went too well," he added. "Too easy. It worries me." He paused a moment then said, "I think I need to talk to Bert."

Hospitable as always, Glenda said, "Why not invite him over here?"

Benny glanced dubiously around the yard and tried to see his guests as he imagined Bert would see them. Two nice but completely clueless citizens; a loose cannon of a woman on the lam; an FBI guy either going rogue or pretending that he was. Benny just didn't think Bert would approve of or enjoy the company, and he hesitated in deciding what to do.

Meg, unasked, suddenly said, "I think calling Bert's a great idea."

The comment only increased Benny's confusion. "You know Bert?"

"We've met," she said casually, pleased with herself for being able to say so. "We've chatted."

"You've chatted," Benny echoed numbly. His world, no less than Sheehan's, seemed to be dissolving and re-forming before his very eyes. Suddenly his wife was playing swim-club games with a Fed. His old friend Bert, an icon of Mafia decorum, was making chitchat with his woo-woo houseguest.

"He's like a Taoist master," Meg put in. "Sometimes he seems to be speaking total gibberish but then he turns out to be right. I think you should call him."

Benny took one more doubtful glance at the people in his swimming pool and yard and then reached for his phone.

36.

"Here's the first thing I don't like," said Bert, who'd installed himself at the shady outdoor table and accepted a tall iced tea from Glenda. He was wearing one of his gorgeous linen shirts with top-stitching on the placket and around the monogrammed chest pocket. He held his chihuahua firmly in his lap for fear it would be clawed to death or eaten by the cat. The little dog's leash was of vermilion canvas; it was the same color as the old man's shirt and the match was not coincidental. "The first thing I don't like," he went on, "is that he changed his mind about hitting you up for cash. Now he's calling it a favor and saying maybe you'll pay it back sometime. Due respect, Benny, why does Carlos need a favor from you? What can you really do for him?"

"That's what I thought, too," said Benny. "But then he says it's a goodwill thing, because, ya know, we may be getting into business on a lease together."

"Right," said Bert. "Getting into business. Business is when money changes hands. This favor stuff is something else."

Benny couldn't disagree but he wanted to present all sides. "So then he says this friend of his, this Benavides, is making a Cuba run anyway, bringing in some things that probably aren't strictly legal, so what's one more piece of cargo?"

"Oh, nice," said Lydia. "Now I'm a piece of cargo."

"What were you expecting?" asked Bert. "A stateroom? But okay, let's take it one thing at a time. Another thing I don't love is where he says the pick-up is. Big Sandy Key? I mean, I understand you don't want to have a bon voyage party right next to the Coast Guard station, but does it really have to be someplace as godforsaken as that? And at midnight?"

"I think that's to do with the moon or the tides or something," Benny said.

Bert said, "I don't think there's even a dock there anymore."

Benny shrugged. "He says that's the place Benavides uses. Knows where the channel is. Has it marked with sticks. Says he can nose the boat right into the mangroves."

Bert slowly stroked his dog. He did this contemplatively, as if he was rubbing his own chin. "Okay, fair enough. Guy's gotta be comfortable where he can bring the boat. But it's just so isolated. And you say Carlos was pretty clear that it should just be you and Lydia?"

"Very clear."

"This I don't like," said Bert, and he went on rhythmically rubbing the dog. After a pause he said, "I dunno, maybe I'm just too cautious. Something like this, I get all hung up in the details, I worry about every little thing. Guess I'm just sort of whaddyacallit, OTB."

"OTB?" said Glenda.

"Ya know, when ya get all fussy about something, ya can't stop thinking about it."

"OCD," said Peter. "OTB is Off-Track Betting."

"Right, whatever. But what I'm saying is I don't like it that he just wants Lydia and Benny and no one else out in a place where's there's no street lights and not even a real road and nothing but mangroves and muck and it doesn't take an Einstein to realize that something bad could happen."

Bert's analysis cast something of a pall over the group. People looked down at their hands or the table or their glasses of iced tea with rivulets of condensation running down the sides. Then Meg said, "But wait a second. None of this is a problem if Carlos is on the level. I mean, none of it's unreasonable. The boat guy's a smuggler, right? He wants a dark place with no extra people around. Why think the worst? I mean, life's nicer if you think positive."

"Nicer but maybe shorter," Bert said. "Look, I don't know what's on Carlos's mind. His people were refugees once. Maybe he's got a soft spot for someone who has to get out of a country. Maybe he just wants to do Benny a solid. It's possible. All I'm saying is that it might maybe be unwise or let's call it imprudent to send two people who are in quite delicate or let's say vulnerable positions off to such a remote and without overstating even a desolate location without some form of support or what would usually be referred to as backup."

"I'll be the backup," Andy Sheehan said without the slightest hesitation.

Bert turned toward him, took a moment to tug on the loose skin beneath his chin while sizing him up. Bert had known some Bureau guys. Some he liked and some he didn't. The ones he liked were tough but not sneaky. When they were after you they let you know it and then they played the game as hard as they could play. They didn't give you high and mighty lectures about right and wrong, they just broke your balls if they could. But they also seemed to understand that without criminals to chase they'd just be bored, suspicious guys in cheap suits. So there was a bond there, a kinship almost. Guys like that you could talk to. Bert said just one word to Sheehan. "Why?"

"Why what?"

"Why are you willing to do backup? What do you want from this?"

"Lydia."

"Like, to arrest her?"

"No, to live with her."

"That's it?"

"That's it."

Bert weighed the words and stared hard at Sheehan. Then he said, "Pet my dog."

"Pet your dog?"

"Pet my dog."

Sheehan gave the chihuahua a perfunctory pat but he kept his gaze firmly locked on Bert as he did so.

Finally Bert said, not to Sheehan but to the group, "Okay, he passes. If a guy uses petting the dog as an excuse to look away from me, I don't trust him. This guy, I think he's okay. But there's still a problem.

A numbers thing. Looking at a worst-case scenario, which is let's face it the type of scenario one often ends up facing in situations such as these, one guy doing backup would probably not be adequate or sufficient to counterbalance any sort of unfair advantage that people of bad faith, if in fact we are dealing with people of bad faith, might wish to have. In other words I think we need to have backup to the backup."

Bert stroked his dog to think. The cat leaped from a standing start into Peter's lap and ignored the chihuahua altogether. A lazy breeze moved through the yard, briefly lifting and agitating fronds and then letting them drop again so that they hung as still as towels on a rack. Peter scratched the cat behind the ears and said, "I have an idea for that."

Everyone was surprised at hearing this from Peter, but no one more so than his wife. She said, "You do?"

Peter said, "Hey, when you're involved, you're involved. Am I right, Bert, or am I right? I've been thinking about this and I think it just might work."

37.

While Bert and Sheehan were driving a dozen or so miles up Highway 1 to reconnoiter the shoreline of Big Sandy Key, Peter made his way through the shrubbery and weeds of the side yard to have a chat with Mel.

He found the old man sitting on his porch, rocking in his creaky chair, picking what was left of his teeth with what seemed to be a corner of a shirt cardboard. As Peter approached the rotting stairs, Mel said, "What? You taking a little breather from the orgy over there?"

"Sorry to disappoint you. There isn't any orgy."

"I see they've invited the Peeper in to join the party. Nice. Pervert shows up, they give him a drink and a babe and everybody's good to go."

Peter said, "Mel, I was hoping to ask a favor."

Mel didn't quite seem to hear that. He said, "Y'ever been to Marseille?"

"No."

"Amazing town, Marseille. I hear they've cleaned it up. I hope not. That would be a shame. Used to be nothing but whorehouses all along the port."

"Must've been very festive," Peter said. "But what I came to ask you—"

"Famous for transvestite hookers. I mean, beautiful. Made these Duval Street queens look like old bags. Some guys—not me, okay?— they'd have a few drinks, zero in on some babe, take her upstairs, reach under the skirt, find a big ol' pair of balls. Then they're all pissed off, like they was tricked, but come on, some of these guys, it's what they wanted all along. Tell me I'm wrong."

"No, I'm sure you're right. But the reason I came over—"

"Me, I never got fooled. I had a policy. No show, no go. I always took a peek right there in the bar. Great town, Marseille."

"And a wise policy," said Peter. "Very wise. But can I please tell you why I stopped by?"

Mel blinked his pale and watery blue eyes and Peter blurted out his favor. Mel sucked his gums and went back to working with the shirt cardboard for a moment, then said, "Well, that's a strange request."

"Yeah, I guess it is a little strange."

The old man broke into a lubricious though mostly toothless smile and lifted his bony chin in the direction of the Bufano house. "Must be getting pretty kinky over there," he said. "I mean, sounds like it's turning kind of rough."

Peter said nothing to that.

"Well, good clean dirty fun," said Mel. "Enjoy it while you can. Doesn't last forever. Except in your mind, I mean. Anyway, what the hell, long as no one's getting hurt."

"Long as no one's getting hurt," said Peter.

Later that afternoon, back at the shady table by the pool, people were looking over Andy Sheehan's shoulder as he drew a rough schematic diagram of Big Sandy Key. The edge of the island was defined by a solid line that didn't satisfy Benny. "Wait a second," he said. "Where are the mangroves?"

"All around," said Sheehan.

"Let's make them look like mangroves, then." He borrowed the pencil and with some deft shading and cross-hatching created a rather convincing impression of the dense, ankle-grabbing plants and the muddled, tangled boundary between oozing land and shallow sea. He was still admiring the effect when Sheehan somewhat testily took back the pencil and resumed his briefing.

Scrawling a large X near the south end of the island, he said, "Here's where the road ends." He drew a couple of smaller X's. "Here are places where you can hide vehicles in the mangroves. Make sure you pull in far enough so there's no light off the back reflectors."

"But not so far that the front end goes down in quicksand," Bert put in. "If you hear sloshing under the hood you've gone too far."

Sheehan drew a circle at the shoreline. "This is the clearing where the boat should come in. There's the remains of an old dock there, you can barely see some pilings sticking out above the surface. So we bushwhack into the mangroves on both sides of the clearing, find spots where we can stay as long as necessary without making a sound. Got it?"

Everybody nodded, though with limited enthusiasm.

"Load up on the bug spray," Sheehan went on. "Wear heavy shoes that the scorpions can't sting through. Gloves would be good for the centipedes and earwigs. Maybe some cotton to stuff in our ears and nostrils. Don't want little things flying in there. Long sleeves for the spiders, high collars for the bats...anything I'm leaving out, Bert?"

"Hats," the old man said. "Hats for the birdshit. Lotsa birds sit out there at night."

"Right," said Sheehan. "Hats for the birdshit. Any questions?"

"Yeah," said Glenda. "Isn't there some less disgusting way to do this?"

"Unfortunately, I don't think so. Any other questions?"

People glanced at one another but there were no further questions. Instead, there was a fraught and lingering silence as the improbable little squad tried to muster the kind of esprit that might ripen into courage, that could make bravery contagious and beat back fear by the simple stratagem of not admitting out loud that fear existed.

Peter broke the quiet with a single word. "Antihistamines."

"What about 'em?" Sheehan said.

"How many can a person take before he falls asleep or goes into a coma? Anybody know?"

"Coma I don't know about," said Bert the Shirt. "But you won't fall asleep, trust me on that. With the frogs, mosquitoes, giant moths, birds crapping and lizards slithering over your feet, there's no way you'll fall asleep."

38.

As the afternoon stretched on, the members of the odd group on Poorhouse Lane oscillated between jumpiness and lethargy. They talked about contingencies and plans, but there really weren't any further plans to make. For a while they sat out by the pool, but there wasn't any horseplay now, no water games, no laughing. The truth was that it was hard for all of them to be together because no one wanted to be the first to admit to nervousness or second thoughts, no one wanted to jinx the group by acknowledging that things could end up going horribly wrong for all of them. Gradually, people drifted away to find some respite. Bert and his chihuahua went home for a nap. Lydia and Sheehan sneaked back to the Last Resort with its misshapen but marvelous bed. Meg and Peter went out for a bike ride.

It was just about an hour before sunset by then. The daylight had mellowed from searing white to buttery yellow and there were long distorted shadows of gnarled tree trunks and the weirdly hand-like outlines of giant leaves stenciled onto the sidewalks and the roofs of cars. The streets still held the heat of noon and the bicycle tires seemed to melt a little bit each time they turned, making a soft sucking sound as they spun against the asphalt. In Bayview Park the drunks lounged on the patchy grass, their ratty backpacks used as pillows. At Higgs Beach the hardcore sun-worshippers swiveled onto their backs for one last blast of tanning on their chests and faces. On White Street Pier stubble-bearded locals were casting bait-nets that gracefully opened into perfect circles and then fell slowly, like parachutes.

Meg and Peter climbed off their bikes at the far end of the pier and blinked out at the twinkling ocean and the green-tinged clouds above the distant reef. Meg said, "This would be a damn nice town for a real vacation. Maybe we should try it sometime."

"Let's get through this one first," said Peter.

"You worried?"

"Of course I am. I'm trying not to let it show. How'm I doing?"

"About as well as any of us." They stood silent for a moment. Offshore, terns were diving, gulls hovering to steal their catch. Meg went on, "We don't have to go through with this, you know."

"I know we don't. Except we sort of do. Don't you agree?"

"Yeah, I do. It's just...it's just that it's so strange, the way it happens."

"The way what happens?"

"Getting to feel responsible for other people," she said. "Other people's problems, screwed up families, pain. It's, like, as soon as you see a right and a wrong, people you root for and people you don't, you're stuck, your gut's already picked a side before your brain has even had time to think it over."

Peter nodded, but distractedly, and gazed off toward the west. The sun was just above the horizon and its light no longer seemed to be filling the entire sky but rather to be focused in a narrow beam that skimmed across the water and pointed straight at anyone who happened to be watching. Without looking down, simply knowing where his wife's hand would be, he took it and said softly, "Meg, I was thinking, the way we are, you and me, it still feels right to you?"

The question startled and baffled her, and she couldn't find an answer right away.

"I mean," he went on, "these other couples...Benny and Glenda, they have screaming fights, crazy break-ups, over-the-top hysterical reunions. Lydia and Sheehan, they're after each other like teenagers, turning their whole lives upside down to be together...You and me, we just sort of undramatically get along, depend on each other, look out for each other."

Meg said, "I think they call that marriage."

"So it's still okay with you?"

She took a deep breath before she answered then let it out slowly to drift off in the mild breeze. "Yeah, it's still okay," she said. "It's more than okay. I can't imagine wanting it any other way. You?"

By way of answer, he took her in his arms and they kissed. The kiss began as a long-married couple's sort of kiss, a casual reminder, a ritual of affection, but in the reddening light of sunset and with the goad of simmering fear for the night ahead, the kiss would not settle for being only that, but deepened and stretched into a new lover's sort of kiss, vibrant with discovery, driven by wonder. They were still embracing as the sun slipped through the horizon and bedded itself in the sea.

39.

By eleven o'clock the unlikely team had re-gathered and dispersed again, leaving only Lydia and Benny behind. At eleven-thirty the two of them walked down the driveway and got into Benny's car.

Seeing the ridiculous plastic hula girl on the dashboard and the handcuffs still dangling from the armrest, Lydia said, "What is it about this car, that whenever I get into it I feel like I'm going God knows where and God knows what will happen?"

Benny said nothing, just started the engine and eased down the narrow street to where it ended at the cemetery.

After a few moments, Lydia said, "You nervous? I'm nervous. Have you ever noticed that some people talk more when they're nervous and some people clam up and hardly talk at all? Anyway, what odds do you give it that we're being set up, double-crossed?"

"Fifty-fifty," Benny said as he turned onto Truman Avenue.

"Now there's a bold prediction. Well, I really hope your buddy Carlos didn't sell us out. Which is kind of weird, because the other day when I thought you were going to kill me, I really didn't care that much. I mean, I cared, I didn't want to die, that's only human, but I didn't *really* care. I didn't like my life that much, I didn't really see it getting better. Now I do. Strange, huh? You live thirty-seven years and nothing really happens. You tack on three more days and everything looks different. Moving to Havana. Falling for a guy."

She paused a moment but there was no response from Benny so she rambled on. "You don't like Sheehan, do you?"

Tactfully, Benny said, "I don't really know him."

"He's difficult to like. That's why I like him. He almost dares you not to. He half wants you to hate him. In fact, he's sort of smug about people hating him, he takes pride in it, it's what gives him his mojo. People are complicated, right? Anyway, it's been a great three extra days. Have I thanked you lately for letting me have them?"

"You don't need to thank me," Benny said. "But do you mind if I turn on the radio? I could use some nice calm music."

The highway turnoff onto Big Sandy Key was marked by a single feeble streetlamp and after that the road was dark. The pavement held out for a mile or so as it wound past a mix of funky cottages and fussily landscaped second homes, then gave way to a rutted single-lane street made of coral chunks and flanked here and there by rusting trailers and shacks propped up on leaning stilts. By imperceptible degrees this roadway slanted downward toward the level of the sea until it spread out like a river delta into a web of side-paths that finally disappeared in mangrove thickets.

At the end of the main track there was a clearing the size of a modest backyard, and in the clearing stood a single large black car with its lights off and its engine running. The car's windows were tinted purple and they reflected hazy points of starlight and the wan gleam of a half-moon that was already slipping down the sky.

Bouncing over coral outcrops, Benny nosed into the clearing and stopped his car. Lydia gave his hand a comradely squeeze before he climbed out. Then he moved around to the passenger side and opened the door that lacked an inside handle.

No one came out of the other vehicle and for a moment the two of them just stood there in the starlight. The air was warm and heavy, it carried a fetid, sulfur smell of low tide. The clearing was still but not quiet; it buzzed with flying insects and rasped with crickets and moaned with frogs and toads.

As their eyes adjusted to the midnight dimness, they saw the vague outline of a boat, a small working craft with a big winch at the stern, tucked into a narrow notch among the mangroves. For some seconds they allowed themselves to imagine that everything was going well and simply, that here was the boat that would carry Lydia to a brand new life in Cuba and leave Benny at home with his wife and his drawings and his secret and his safety.

A rear door opened in the big black car. A wedge of yellow light stretched then shrank away as Carlos climbed out and closed the door behind him. He was, as always, dressed in perfect clothes, pressed and pleated, elegant as an expensive knife. He moved toward Lydia and Benny on small feet in beautiful shoes. When he was just a step away, he looked Lydia up and down and said, "So, this is the lovely refugee."

With an odd formality, as though in a workplace, she extended her hand for a shake that Carlos shied away from. She went on with her introduction anyway. "Lydia Greenspan. I just want to—"

"Just want to what?" he interrupted. "Thank me? A gracious thought, but premature. Don't thank me yet. Let me show you to your accommodations." And with a sweeping Old World gesture, he pointed the way toward the notch in the mangroves.

40.

They moved at a measured pace across the clearing, Lydia walking first, Benny, feeling misgivings at the backs of his knees, forcing his feet to follow. The waxy mangroves in front of them drank up the faint light and threw back a more viscous darkness. As they drew closer to the soupy boundary between land and water, the riot of bugs grew louder and the stink of rot got stronger. The hard ground was just giving way to muck when a shadow suddenly moved and assumed the shape of a man. The shadow took on mass and volume as it raised a .44 magnum that glinted dully in the moonlight and was pointed at the level of Lydia's heart.

She froze in mid-step, unbalanced, nearly stumbling forward. Benny, ashamed to let her shield him, stepped out to the side, tried to cross in front. She stopped him with an arm.

From behind them, Carlos said, "You see? It's just as well you didn't thank me. I won't be sending you to Cuba. For a boat ride, yes. Both of you. But only as far as the outside of the reef. Where the big sharks hang out, at the drop-off. Feeding on the little fish that wander out too deep. Like you."

Benny stammered out, "But why--?"

Almost pityingly, Carlos said, "Benny. Benny. You call yourself a businessman, but you know nothing about business. You know nothing about anything. Why would I do a favor for you when I could do one for a man who actually matters?"

He gestured back toward the dark car. Frank Fortuna was just climbing out of it and he stood now in the wedge of light that escaped through the open door, his leonine hair gleaming, his heavy jaw and thick neck silhouetted. Slowly, with what he imagined would pass for dignity, he walked across the clearing, approached his son-in-law, and spat in his face.

"You disgust me, Benny," he said. "For years I protected you, thought of you almost like a son. Then I ask you to do one simple job. I ask you to protect me for once, against some bitch who's about to turn on me—"

"I wasn't about to turn on you, you stupid bastard," Lydia cut in.

Fortuna ignored her as if she were already drowned. "—And you're not man enough to do it. You run. You hide. You're soft, Benny, a total disappointment." To the man with the magnum, he said, "Go ahead, sink these two, get 'em out of my sight."

The man waved the .44, gave Lydia a quick prod with the muzzle, started nudging the captives over the last few feet of squishing ground toward the waiting boat.

But before they reached it there was an abrupt clattering in the mangroves and a tall figure burst through. His clothing was buttoned up from head to toe as though for jungle combat and his gun was braced across his wrist. He shouted, "Drop it!"

The man with the magnum didn't. They faced off, one on one, not much more than a stride apart.

Frank Fortuna said, "And who the fuck are you?"

"Special Agent Andrew Sheehan, FBI." He said it without ever moving his eyes.

"FBI," Fortuna said, as though naming a disease. It seemed to take him just a heartbeat to size up the situation and then he threw a look of quiet fury at Carlos. "You set me up, you little prick?"

Carlos blanched, his perfect clothes seemed suddenly to wilt. "No! I swear to God."

The silver-haired man spun his gaze toward Lydia, looked at her with utter hate. "So it had to be the bitch. Sure, you weren't about to turn—"

"I didn't turn," she said. "I told you that."

The two men with the guns kept their eyes glued to one another and their fingers gradually grew more taut around the triggers.

"Everything that's happened, Frank," Lydia went on, "you know why it happened? It all started because you called a hit on me. And why'd you do that? Because you lost your nerve."

"Bullshit, I lost my nerve."

"You lost it, Frank. I asked for a raise, you got all paranoid. Paranoid and cheap and selfish. You're so selfish, so puffed up with your stupid pride, you'd kill your own daughter's husband."

Fortuna was unmoved by that. He glanced dismissively at Benny and said, "So what? I found her this bum. I'll find her someone better."

"Like hell you will."

The shrill and simple words came disembodied from the mangroves, and in the next instant, accompanied by the snap of breaking twigs, Glenda came hurtling through the foliage, her eyes wild and inflamed with bug bites, her tall shoes muddy, her hair matted here and there with cobwebs. "You're done running my life," she shouted at her father. "There's one man who's important to me. Benny. Not you. I don't need anything from you. I don't want anything from you."

Trying not to show that he was stung, Fortuna said, "You're out of control, Glenda. We'll talk about this when you're calmer. When you understand the world a little better."

"We'll talk about it now," she said. "I don't care if I ever see you again. Not even in prison."

That was an unspeakable word in the Fortuna family. Saying it now was meant to wound, and it did. Glenda's father absorbed it and frowned down at the soggy ground a moment. But then, after several heartbeats, the frown curled itself into a very nasty hint of a smile and his eyes slid away from Glenda, back toward the far end of the clearing. At last he said in a softly gloating tone, "Prison? I don't think we need to talk about prison here. Look behind you, Mr. FBI."

41.

Too experienced to be decoyed, Sheehan swiveled only slightly, always keeping the first shooter in view. But it turned out that Fortuna wasn't bluffing. Two more men, stubby revolvers drawn and wagging, were stepping gingerly but relentlessly across the coral slabs and knobs. One of them was Mikey Ferraro, Benny's former pal. The other was the goon who'd thrown Peter off the seawall.

With quiet satisfaction, Fortuna watched his allies approach, and as soon as he was sure the advantage had swung his way again, he reverted to his usual stance of taunter and bully. "You're outgunned, my friend," he said to Sheehan. "Three to one. They teach you how to deal with that in cop school?"

Sheehan didn't answer, just slowly panned his weapon back and forth among his adversaries.

To Carlos, Fortuna said, "That tub of yours. Room for one more body?"

"No problem. Short ride."

"Strange," Fortuna mused to Sheehan, "that the Bureau would put you out here all alone. No snipers? No helicopters? No SWAT team? What is it, a budget issue?"

"No, it's a do the right thing issue."

The words seemed to come forth from the night itself but the voice that spoke them was vaguely though hauntingly familiar to Fortuna.

In the next instant there was a scuffling in the mangroves as of a small stampede, branches slapping, feet sloshing through shallow stagnant puddles. Shakily but without hesitation an old man emerged from the thicket. He wore a wide-brimmed hat that was splattered with guano and a monogrammed teal silk shirt pricked here and there by thorns; he had wispy streamers of absorbent cotton protruding from his ears and nose and an M-14 was braced against his stiff and bony shoulder.

Seeming to be caught between believing and disbelieving in a ghost, Fortuna said, "Bert? You old bastard. You're still alive?"

"Just barely. Alive enough to know that no one but a cheap punk from Staten Island would call a hit against a woman. You oughta be ashamed."

"And you oughta be embalmed. Stay out of this, old man. It's no concern of yours, and anyway, you're still one gun too few."

"Says you."

He moved a half-step aside and two more spattered and bug-bitten figures spilled out of the mangroves. One of them was Meg, who was brandishing an Uzi. The other was Peter and he was tracing little circles with an AK-47. "I count four to three," Bert went on. "Ours are automatic."

Fortuna blinked toward the new arrivals in their preposterous jungle get-ups. "Jesus Christ. Who the fuck are you people?"

Peter shrugged so that the muzzle of his gun bobbed up and down. "Um, we're here on a home exchange."

"A home exchange? A fucking home exchange?"

Meg hardened down with her trigger finger. "But we'll do what we gotta do. Don't fuck with us, Frank."

He made a mollifying gesture, just a small one, not to be mistaken for surrender.

Bert said, "Listen, we're not here to bust your balls. All we want is a fair shake for Lydia and Benny. We're gonna offer you a deal."

Fortuna said, "A deal? A deal from an ancient has-been and two nobodies with cotton up their nose?"

"It make you feel better, insulting people?" Bert asked him. "You wanna hear the offer or you want we start shooting?"

Fortuna did a quick scan of his forces. They didn't look too eager to face the automatics. He said, "Go 'head, let's hear the deal."

Bert started to speak, then swallowed instead and said somewhat sheepishly, "Shit, I can't remember the details. Peter here is gonna lay it out."

Peter said, "I am?"

There was a silence. It stretched on as hard shoes began to paw impatiently at the soggy ground.

Lydia said, "Come on, Peter, like we talked it through this afternoon."

He was trying but he couldn't quite get his voice to work. He looked at the man with the magnum and the men with the revolvers and he couldn't help feeling extremely worried. The worry formed a dense mass that lodged in his throat like a too big bite of steak.

His wife whispered to him, "Come on, honey, you can do it. I know you can."

She lightly leaned her shoulder against his. The familiar contact unfroze something and the words began to flow. "Okay," he said, "okay. So here we are, Frank."

"Right, asshole, here we are."

Peter soldiered on. "There's you, there's us, and the way I see it, there's three choices here. Choice one, we have a bloody, gory, messy shootout and everybody dies. But that doesn't have to happen."

"Go on," Fortuna said.

"Choice two. No one shoots. Sheehan takes you into custody and you go to jail, probably for quite a while. That doesn't have to happen either."

"I'm listening," said the silver-haired man. "So what's behind door number three?"

Peter stalled a beat, but now it wasn't because he was afraid to speak. It was because, to his own amazement, he was suddenly savoring the confrontation. What the hell was going on? He was living on the very edge and he found he sort of liked it. Softly, but in a firmer tone, he said, "All right, choice three. First off, absolution for Benny. You don't touch him, ever. You never ask anything of him again. For all intents and purposes, he's no longer in the Mob."

"I can't just do that. He took the oath—"

"Fuck the oath!" Bert the Shirt put in. "All of a sudden the woman-killer's a stickler for the rules. You let him go, unofficially of course, he's gone. Agreed?"

Before Fortuna could answer, Peter shocked himself further by improvising. "And he gets a year's free rent on a gallery. Courtesy of Carlos. To make up for being a double-crossing scumbag."

Carlos said, "Now wait a second—"

"Shut up," said Fortuna. To Peter he said, "Go on, let's hear the rest."

Peter made him wait a little bit. "The rest is that you pay Lydia and Sheehan to keep quiet and to leave the country. Two million bucks should do it."

"Two million bucks! But that's, that's—"

"I think it's called a shakedown, Frank," said Meg, making little circles with her gun.

"It's actually a bargain," Peter said. "Very fair. Solves everybody's problems."

"I don't see where it solves dick," Fortuna said.

Calmly, Peter said, "That's because you haven't thought it out. I have. Sheehan need six more months to get a pension He can use that time to have you put away and go out in a blaze of glory. Or he can quit next week if the same money happens to appear in a lump sum. Say, in a safe deposit box in New York."

"Right. I'm out two mil and this bullshit's still hanging over me."

"No, it won't be," Peter said. "Here's the nice part. You get a receipt--"

"A receipt? A fucking receipt? Why am I even listening to this crap?"

"--In the form of some very incriminating photos that Sheehan took of Lydia with your crooked broker."

"Great. They get two million. I get some snapshots."

"Frank, I don't think you're paying your best attention right now. You're missing the nuances."

"Don't tell me what I'm missing."

"The pictures, Frank. Evidence. They're selling you evidence. You can prove it. So you've got Lydia for blackmail and Sheehan for soliciting bribes. Just like they have you for insider trading and murder conspiracy. Nobody can squeal because everybody's guilty. Life goes on. Tidy, right? Whaddya say, Frank? Deal?"

42.

It was after 2 am by the time the unlikely allies had all straggled back to the Bufano house, but no one even thought about sleeping. They were too wired from the face-off and too itchy from the mangroves. Except for Bert, they'd stripped down to their underwear and jumped into the pool. Bert sat on the apron with his pale feet and scaly shins dangling in the water. With one hand he rather apologetically caressed his dog, which had been left alone for an unusually long time, and with the other he rubbed his aching joints. "Man," he said, "I'm getting a little old for this shit."

"Like hell you are," said Glenda, and reached him the bottle of their very best aged tequila that was being passed from wet hand to wet hand.

He took a swig and smacked his big lips in appreciation. "Worth it, though," he said. To Benny, he went on, "You're a free man now, my friend. No more nasty errands, nothing you can't say no to. How's it feel?"

Before he answered, Benny pinched his nose, dunked full-length, and came up sweeping back his sparse hair so that droplets flew like shooting stars in the soft blue light. "Feels amazing. Feels about a hundred pounds lighter." He took his turn with the bottle and then, in an upwelling of good-fellowship, he said to Sheehan, "And you're a free man, too. No more bosses, no more bullshit politics. How's it feel for you?"

The agent's reaction wasn't nearly so effusive. "The truth?" he said. "The truth is I'm all mixed up. I just let a bad guy get away. Twenty years, I've never done that. How'm I supposed to feel? Pass that bottle over here...You know what it is? I feel guilty that I don't feel guilty. I should feel guilty, right? I just let myself be bought."

"And you got a damn good price," said Lydia. "Two million bucks and me and a whole new life in Paris."

"Paris? I thought we were going to Havana?"

"I changed my mind. Get used to it, Sheehan."

A moment passed, then, as sometimes happened, Bert's mind wandered back to a subject that others in the conversation seemed finished with. "Guilty, not guilty," he said. "Ya did right, ya did wrong. It's a whaddyacallit, a paragon—"

"Paradox," said Peter.

"Right, there's different ways ya can look at it. By the rulebook, okay, ya did wrong. Get over it. 'Cause say ya did the boy scout thing and Fortuna got sent away. Ya don't think guys call hits from prison? Ya don't think there woulda been revenge? Besides, there's the family thing. Never overlook that. The guy may be a bastard but he's still Glenda's father."

"You had to remind me?" she said.

"And I don't care what an awful guy he is," Bert went on, "I just don't think anybody wants to see their old man go to jail. Do you, Glenda? Tell the truth."

She'd drenched her hair to get the bugs and cobwebs out of it; it lay flat against her head and framed her face, which had been rinsed of all but a few random smears of make-up. She looked young. She looked like someone's daughter. She said, "No, I guess not. Would've made things easier in a way, given me an excuse to cut him off. But I don't think that would've felt right. Where's that tequila?...Thing is, something really strange happened while we were standing there in the muck. I realized something, sort of for the first time. He'll be an old man soon. I don't need him anymore, he's gonna need me. Man, it's weird the first time you look at your father and think that."

There was a quiet moment then. The pool pump softly hummed. A scrap of breeze folded back the palm fronds and let them fall again, pinpricks of starlight being revealed or blotted as the foliage was rearranged. Crickets rasped and paused, and during one of the pauses Bert the Shirt could be heard gruffly chuckling and talking to his dog.

"The bit with the fake guns, Nacho, ya shoulda seen it. That was really pretty good."

"They weren't fake," said Meg, "just a little bent and rusty. Some shoe polish and WD-40, they looked just fine."

"Yeah, they looked great," Bert said. "Who's arguing? But the others guys' guns could shoot. I mean, for instance, they had bullets. Pulling off that bluff, that took balls. Stroke'a genius, Peter."

Peter tingled at the compliment but said nothing.

"Always thought of you as kind of a nervous guy," Bert went on. "Jumpy. A little neurotic, no offense. Then you stand out there and pull that off. That showed me something. Were you worried?"

"Worried? Nah. Not at all. More like scared shitless. My turn with the bottle." Fearful of germs, he discreetly wiped the rim before he sipped. "Terrified," he went on, "except for around two minutes, when I totally wasn't. Wish I knew how it happened. Some people have anxiety attacks, right? Me, I had a fit of calm. Perfect calm. Didn't last, of course. When Fortuna finally drove away I just about fainted. But while that feeling lasted it was amazing."

"You had a glimpse of Nirvana," said his wife.

"Let's not push it. I didn't soil myself, that's a win."

"Come on," said Bert, "give yourself some credit. Scared, not scared, it doesn't matter how ya felt. It matters what ya did. And what ya did out there was very brave." The bottle had come his way again and he lifted it toward Peter as a toast. *"Salud."*

Muffled echoes of the festive word came from all around the swimming pool, but then Benny said in a darker tone, "But wait. Just wait. I got one big problem with all of this."

The group hushed. The little splashes and gurgles in the water subsided.

"I mean," he went on, "look, everything's great. I got my life back, I'm with Glenda, I even get a chance to see if anybody likes my drawing. But what's really bothering me right now is that, Meg and Peter, you've done so much for us and I have no idea how I can ever pay you back."

"Pay it forward," said Meg, then added a little tipsily, "Does anybody actually know exactly what the hell that means?"

"I'd just feel better," Benny said, "if there was something I could do for you, something I could give you. Something. Anything. Name it."

Peter looked at Meg. Meg looked at Peter. They shared a wonderful moment of realizing there was nothing that they lacked, nothing that they craved, nothing that was missing from their life together. Then, over his wife's shoulder, Peter saw Tasha the Burmese cat crouched under a lounge chair, looking at him adoringly, her yellow eyes gathering up an improbable intensity of starlight and sending it back his way. He said at last, "Um, maybe there's just one thing."

"Name it," Benny said. "Anything. It's yours."

"Nah," said Peter, "I couldn't ask."

Epilogue

He didn't ask, but as soon as they got back to New York Peter started calling shelters, looking for a Burmese cat. One of the shelter workers said to him, "It has to be a Burmese?"

"Yes. They're hypoallergenic."

"No they're not. Whatever gave you that idea?"

Peter looked at Meg. Meg sort of shrugged. Peter said to the shelter lady, "Well, it has to be a Burmese anyway."

Eventually they got one, a neutered male. In honor of Tasha they named it Sasha. At first, Peter made the fundamental error of trying to befriend the cat, and the cat, heartbreakingly, seemed to despise him. Peter then forced himself for some days to ignore the animal and even lightly to kick at it and hiss if it came nearby. Sasha was soon drinking water from the kitchen faucet and purring in its master's lap as he sat reading in the little alcove with the globe in it.

At the FBI office in Queens, rumors swirled about the sudden shocking resignation of Andy Sheehan. Six months from a pension, why would anyone do anything except show up, punch the clock, and keep his head down? There had to be some dark secret, some scandal brewing. Sheehan cited personal reasons for departing and left it, officially, at that. The only person to whom he confided even a bit more information was his old friend Lou Duncan, who came in as Sheehan was in the midst of the brief, bleak chore of clearing out his office.

"I just don't get it," Duncan said. "You go to Florida full of piss and vinegar. You're going to break a case that isn't even yours and come back a conquering hero. Instead you come back with a tan and quit. What changed?"

"Everything."

"That's a little vague," said Duncan.

Sheehan kept on with his clearing. Without looking up he said, "Okay, I met someone and I stopped being sure what I believed in. And I'm not even sure which happened first."

"Met someone. Like, a woman?"

"We're moving to Rome."

"Italy or Georgia?"

"Italy. Unless she changes her mind again. It was going to be Havana, then Paris. She's amazing, I've never known anybody like her."

"Paris, Rome," mused Duncan. "You without a pension. Guess she has some money, huh?"

Sheehan kept his eyes on his desk. "Rich uncle. Decent inheritance."

Duncan said, "That's good, because you lost your bet."

"Bet?"

Duncan laughed. "You damn sure would have remembered if you won. You didn't nab your man. You owe a hundred bucks to Catholic Charities."

"Shit," the tall man said. "You're right. I do."

In Key West, Benny opened up his rent-free gallery and took to wearing a tropic-weight beret that covered up his bald spot. His drawings sold for modest prices; some weeks nothing sold at all. Benny didn't mind. He set up his easel in a space at the back and the hours just flew by.

The rest of winter passed, as did spring and summer. On a whim, Glenda had planted the death-threat coconut in a corner of the yard and it sprouted quickly in the soaking rains and steamy heat. By October the shoot was six feet tall.

Meg and Glenda kept in touch, and in November they talked about exchanging homes over Christmas. To the Bufanos, the lights and pageantry and bustling crowds of Manhattan at Christmastime sounded fabulous; to the Kaplans, a warm-weather break before the onslaught of another northern winter seemed divine. But at the last minute there was a complication. Glenda was in the middle of her first trimester and not feeling well enough to travel. She suggested that her friends come stay with them instead.

This worried Peter. What if the two cats didn't get along?

"Last trip we faced live ammo," Meg reminded him. "Now you're worried about a cat fight?"

Glenda was persistent. "Please," she urged. "Take back your old guest room. Have a real vacation this time around. No guns, no home invasions, no broken windows."

Meg and Peter finally agreed.

On Christmas Eve, Glenda invited a couple of old friends to join them for a Feast of Seven Fishes. There was salt cod and shrimp, and of course there was cracked conch and conch fritters. Old Mel from next door told highly inappropriate stories of Yuletides spent in low bordellos. Bert the Shirt, his chihuahua nestled in his lap against the feared predation of the cats, reminisced about cooking holiday suppers in small kitchens with his wife, him darting back and forth shucking clams and breading flounder while she danced past him, usually singing opera, with steaming colanders of pasta.

There was another guest as well. He mostly hung back in conversation, not, it seemed, from shyness, but because he now understood that this was not his house and not his party. Frank Fortuna's daughter was about to present him with a grandchild, and this simple wondrous fact somehow humbled him, resigned him not with rancor but relief to the ebb and flow of power in families and in life, called forth an unselfish tenderness that he had fallen short of acting on when he'd first become a father, back when he was so much younger. He brought gifts for everyone and hugged not only Glenda, but Benny also, when he left.

Meg and Peter stayed at the Bufano house until just after New Year's. During that time almost nothing happened, and it was blissful. There was sun, there was beach, there was salt water still warm as skin from the high heat of summer. The only drama lay in watching Key West fill up for the tourist season, its streets and bars and porches swelling with visitors in loud shirts. Day by day, hour by hour, pale people flooded in by plane, by car, by boat, vast flocks heading southward and absolutely no one heading north.

Even so, there were places on the island that never seemed crowded, and one of them was White Street Pier. Meg and Peter rode there on bicycles every day an hour or so before the sun went down. This soon became more than just a habit; it took on the significance of ritual, the sanctity of a tradition.

Stepping off their bikes, kicking down their kickstands just like kids, they watched the locals with their fishing poles and bait nets, the distant sailboats moored out near the reef, and they savored, as human beings have forever, the ancient and still fresh suspense of the sun's slow dive into the sea. When it touched the horizon they held hands and when it had settled beneath the faintly rippling surface they kissed. By the time their eyes were open again the western sky had paled to yellow-green and there was a coppery sheen on the ocean.

ABOUT THE AUTHOR

Laurence Shames has been a New York City taxi driver, lounge singer, furniture mover, lifeguard, dishwasher, gym teacher, and shoe salesman. Having failed to distinguish himself in any of those professions, he turned to writing full-time in 1976 and has not done an honest day's work since.

His basic laziness notwithstanding, Shames has published more than twenty books and hundreds of magazine articles and essays. Best known for his critically acclaimed series of Key West novels, he has also authored non-fiction and enjoyed considerable though largely secret success as a collaborator and ghostwriter. Shames has penned four New York Times bestsellers. These have appeared on four different lists, under four different names, none of them his own. This might be a record.

Born in Newark, New Jersey in 1951, to chain-smoking parents of modest means but flamboyant emotions, Shames graduated summa cum laude from NYU in 1972 and was inducted into Phi Beta Kappa. Shortly after finishing college, he began annoying editors by sending them short stories they hated. He also wrote longer things he thought of as novels. He couldn't sell them.

By 1979 he'd somehow passed himself off as a journalist and was publishing in top-shelf magazines like Playboy, Outside, Saturday Review, and Vanity Fair. In 1982, Shames was named Ethics columnist of Esquire, and also made a contributing editor to that magazine.

By 1986 he was writing non-fiction books whose critical if not commercial success first established his credentials as a collaborator/ghostwriter. His 1991 national bestseller, BOSS OF BOSSES, written with two FBI agents, got him thinking about the Mafia. It also bought him a ticket out of New York and a sweet little house in Key West, where he finally got back to Plan A: writing fiction. Given his then-current preoccupations, the novels--beginning with FLORIDA STRAITS--naturally featured palm trees, high humidity, dogs in sunglasses, and blundering New York mobsters.

Having had the good fortune to find a setting he loved and a wonderfully loyal readership as well, Shames wrote eight Key West novels during the 1990s, before taking a decade-long detour into screenwriting and collaborative work. In 2013, he returned to his favorite fictional turf with SHOT ON LOCATION--a suspenseful and hilarious mix of Hollywood glitz and Florida funky.

TROPICAL SWAP, Shames' tenth Key West novel, tells the riotous tale of a home exchange that sounds too good to be true, and is.

Made in the USA
Lexington, KY
08 March 2016